"I'll welcome you as a daughter."

Edward Knight squeezed Jenny's hands reassuringly. "And the friction between my sons will eventually smooth out."

"You don't understand." Jenny spoke in a rush. "He doesn't want to marry me."

"You're mistaken," Mr. Knight insisted. "I've never seen Tony so—"

"I don't love Tony!" It was a cry of torment. "Not in the way he wants. That's what makes it so hard."

"It's Robert." He sighed and smiled at Jenny with pure, undiluted pleasure. "I had grave doubts for a successful marriage between you and Tony. But Robert is a different proposition."

Jenny was completely bewildered. He was acting as if everything were all right.

"Ah, yes!" he exclaimed with satisfaction. "That changes the complexion of things. Robert is no romantic fool. What w— masterly c— chess, my d—

Books by Emma Darcy

EMMA DARCY

song of a wren

Harlequin Books

TORONTO • NEW YORK • LONDON
AMSTERDAM • PARIS • SYDNEY • HAMBURG
STOCKHOLM • ATHENS • TOKYO • MILAN

Harlequin Presents first edition March 1986
ISBN 0-373-10864-8

Original hardcover edition published in 1985
by Mills & Boon Limited

CHAPTER ONE

IT was mid-afternoon when they reached the outskirts of Sydney. Jenny's former visits to the city had all been by train and she found the heavy traffic and the driving habits of the motorists rather unnerving. Everyone seemed bent on competing for the fastest run into the city and Tony was certainly not loath to pick up the challenge. He free-wheeled the van from lane to lane with a reckless disregard for thundering semi-trailers and charging buses. Jenny gasped in horror when he defied the might of an oncoming Mack truck to squeeze into a gap on the outside lane.

He threw her a triumphant grin. 'Relax. Like Brer Rabbit, I was born and bred in this blackberry patch and I've yet to dent a fender.'

'If you keep driving like this, all your Christmases will come at once,' Jenny retorted feelingly.

Tony laughed and reached across to give her hand a reassuring squeeze. 'Not to worry, Jenny-wren. We're on the home stretch now.'

It was all right for him, Jenny thought wryly. Tony never worried about anything. She slanted him a look of affectionate exasperation. Her lodger. He was more like a perennial ray of sunshine with his cheerful personality and beach-boy looks. He had swept into her life, brushing aside the greyness of her existence as well as all the arguments that he was not the kind of person Jenny had envisaged when she had advertised for someone to share her house. A handsome footloose artist was certainly not a woman schoolteacher, but the decision to let him stay had been the best decision she had ever made.

Her mouth curved into a self-mocking smile. Who was she kidding? Tony had made the decision. She had just found herself going along with him. Somehow he could always manoeuvre her into doing what he wanted. Like this invitation to spend Christmas with his family. She had not wanted to accept, had not intended to accept, but here she was on her way with him. Almost there. And perhaps it would be better than spending Christmas alone with grieving memories of her father.

As if he had caught her thoughts Tony turned to her with his winning smile. 'We're going to have a great Christmas, Jenny. Always do at our house but having you with me will make it even better. You'll be one of the family in no time at all. I can hardly wait to show you off.'

'So I noticed,' she said dryly and smiled in response, but as he returned his attention to the road Jenny's smile took on an ironic twist.

No way was she going to feel at home with his extraordinary family, but she was curious to meet them. Tony took their achievements for granted but Jenny had lived most of her life in the small coastal township of Nangoa and such remarkable people were far outside her acquaintance.

At first she had wondered if Tony was pulling her leg whenever he tossed off some information about his family but gradually she had come to accept that he was speaking the absolute truth. His father was a publishing magnate. His mother was a successful artist who specialised in illustrating children's books. Jenny had seen some of them in the Nangoa library. His older brother, Robert, did indeed produce and direct variety and musical shows for television. Miranda, his sister, was an up-and-coming actress, and from all school reports, his younger brother, Peter, was a mathematical genius.

In such company Jenny was sure she would feel hopelessly out of place, but she had reasoned that Tony's familiar and amiable presence would ease the awkwardness of fitting in. With a deft turn of the wheel, Tony steered the van off the freeway and jolted her out of her introspection.

Hunter's Hill was one of the older settlements on the north shore of the harbour and Jenny looked around with interest. The streets were narrow and for the most part they were lined with old, gnarled trees, their foliage thick with many years of pruning. Homes were set well back behind their fences, almost hidden by gardens which had been established for generations. Overall there was an impressive air of quiet dignity.

'Here we are!' Tony announced, turning the van into a gravelled driveway.

Jenny gaped at the huge frontage of a two-storeyed home which spread behind groves of trees and manicured lawns. It looked as if a piece of Tudor England had been cut out and set down in this hideaway corner, totally eccentric in this most Australian of Australian cities. Tony had spoken of his home as a great barn of a place, completely neglecting to mention that it was a barn of style and character.

She should have been prepared for this, Jenny berated herself silently. It stood to reason that the Knight family had to be wealthy but the sudden confrontation with the substance of their wealth was a shock nevertheless. All her misgivings about this visit returned in full measure as Tony braked the van to a halt at the entrance steps.

He bounded out, opened her door, took the steps in a couple of strides and leaned on the doorbell. 'Come on, Jenny-wren. Shake a leg,' he called excitedly.

This Jenny-wren wants to fly home to Nangoa, she thought as she forced her legs to move. An insignificant little bird did not belong here and never would.

But she was trapped now. Already a woman had opened the door, a tall, statuesque woman, grey-haired but still retaining the confident glow of beauty which had always been hers. The lines of experience only accentuated it. Tony ignored the dignity of age, sweeping the woman into his arms and swinging her off her feet in an exuberant hug.

Jenny sighed and walked up the steps. The Knights were only people, she told herself sternly. She was a person, wasn't she? Tony was here and she was an invited guest. There was no reason to panic.

'Tony! Put me down. Will you ever grow up?' came the laughing protest.

'I'm all grown, Mum. Haven't you noticed?' he retorted, putting his mother down and holding her at arm's length so that she could see all of him.

Instead of taking the notice demanded she turned a smiling gaze to Jenny. 'I suppose it's useless to expect Tony to act sensibly. Welcome to our home, Jenny.'

Why, she's just like Tony, Jenny thought in surprised relief. There was youth and laughter in the blue eyes and generosity in the wide, smiling mouth. Jenny's heart warmed to the obvious welcome on the older woman's face. 'Thank you, Mrs Knight. It's very kind of you to have me.'

It surprised Jenny even further to have her hands taken in a gesture of open acceptance.

'My dear, it's always a pleasure to meet friends of my children, and Tony so rarely brings anyone home it is doubly a pleasure. You must be a very special girl.'

'Sure is, Mum,' Tony grinned, winking at Jenny as he hung a possessive arm around her shoulder. 'She's my very special live-in lady.'

'Tony!' She reproved him with a foot-jab to the ankle.

'Ow! See how she keeps me in line?' he howled, pretending injury but still keeping up his outrageous fiction.

Jenny's cheeks burned with embarrassment. She could barely meet his mother's eyes. 'Mrs Knight, Tony does share my house but he doesn't share my . . .' She stopped, wishing she could bite off her wayward tongue.

Annabel Knight laughed and drew Jenny's arm through hers. 'Come inside. You must want a drink after that long drive. It's been so hot today. You can unpack later.'

'Your sitting-room, Mum,' Tony directed. 'I can have a squint in the studio while you talk to Jenny.'

His mother sighed and gave Jenny a pained look. 'Maybe one day he'll learn to be civilised.'

Jenny grinned. 'Not when he's painting or can look at paintings.'

'I can see you know him well,' came the dry retort. 'I understand that you're a music teacher,' she added with a look of speculative interest.

'That's right. Piano, organ and guitar.'

'And she sings,' Tony added. 'I want Rob to hear her.'

'Well he won't,' Jenny said emphatically, shooting Tony a mutinous look. They had already had this argument when he had put her guitar in the van.

'Why not, Jenny? Robert is always interested in new talent,' his mother said kindly.

'That's just it, Mrs Knight. I've no great talent and I'm certainly no performer. It would only be an embarrassment to me and to him if I sang for Tony's brother. Compared to the people Robert is dealing with all the time I am a rank amateur, and believe me, I do know my limitations.'

'Limitations!' Tony scoffed. 'She's better than anything I've seen or heard on Rob's musical shows. Bet you agree with me, Mum.'

They had walked down a tall-ceilinged hallway which seemed dark after the brilliant sunshine outside. The sitting-room they entered was bathed in light. One wall was completely glassed and the opposite wall was a virtual gallery of paintings. The parquet flooring was strewn with thick, shaggy mats and loose-cushioned armchairs gave the room a casual atmosphere. The paintings were fascinating, pure childhood fantasy, brilliantly coloured and executed in meticulous detail.

Jenny stood in front of them, completely enraptured. 'They're so beautiful,' she murmured. 'I've seen your work in books but . . .' She glanced her appreciation at Annabel Knight, unable to express exactly what she felt. She surprised a look of understanding pass between mother and son.

'Have you tried?'

'I've tried,' Tony replied with an edge of frustration. 'But I haven't completely caught it. Not yet anyway.'

'Elusive effect,' his mother nodded. Then seeing Jenny's bewilderment she smiled. 'Sorry, my dear. It's your face, you see. An artist would give his eye-teeth to capture it in oils.'

'My face!' Jenny cried in astonishment. 'But it's so ordinary!'

'Would that we could see ourselves as others see us,' Annabel Knight muttered in amusement. 'Please forgive us for talking shop and do sit down and relax. Tony, there's a jug of Christmas punch in the refrigerator. Do the honours before you disappear into the studio.'

There was a small utilitarian bar in one corner. A refrigerator, sink and electric kettle obviously provided conveniences for Annabel Knight when she was working. An archway led from the sitting-room into the studio. This was a long room running out from the body of the house and it was glassed on all three sides.

Tony's mother had obviously followed Jenny's

gaze. 'I do all my work here. Unlike Tony, I don't traipse around the countryside to find scenes to paint. It all comes out of my imagination. How do you cope with all his artist's clutter in your house?'

'It's not in the house. It's in the toolshed.'

'I converted it into a studio,' Tony explained as he handed them tall glasses of punch. 'That's how we first met. I fell in love with her toolshed and propositioned her. You can have me if I can have your toolshed, I said. But would you believe? She actually wanted rent-money.'

'I'd advertised for a lodger,' Jenny put in hurriedly, shaking her head at Tony in exasperation. 'And if you keep talking like that, Tony, your mother will think we're living in sin.'

He grinned unashamedly. 'Jenny-wren, my mother has only to take one look at those lovely, luminous eyes of yours and the truth is laid bare for her.'

A self-conscious blush rose to her cheeks as he turned to walk into the studio. Jenny did not consider her eyes lovely at all. They were an unremarkable hazel-brown. And she did not fancy the idea that she was as transparent as Tony claimed. Heaven alone knew what his mother thought. The older woman's hand reached across and patted Jenny's. She looked up into warm, kindly eyes.

'He likes you very much,' came the knowing comment.

'I like him too,' Jenny replied in a rush of relief. 'He's been wonderful company for me these last six months, so kind and cheerful.'

'Tony said you have no family, Jenny.' The

words were soft, sympathetic, gently raising the question.

'My father died this year, a few months before Tony came. He had been ill for a long time, in a wheelchair these last years. Dad insisted that I finish my studies at the Conservatorium of Music but since then I've always taught music from home so I could be at hand. I know it was a release for him when he died but I miss him terribly at times.'

'I'm sure you must do.' She hesitated, then asked tentatively, 'And your mother?'

'I didn't really know her. She died when I was three. Dad brought me up. He was a wonderful father.'

'So now you're alone.'

'Yes.' The talk of family had re-awakened Jenny's doubts about accepting Tony's invitation. A thread of anxiety ran through her voice as she added, 'Mrs Knight, I know Christmas is family-time. Tony wouldn't take no for an answer. I do hope I won't be too much in the way here.'

Annabel Knight gave her a piercing look. Then her features softened and she took Jenny's hand in a warm grasp. 'My dear, you don't know what a marvellous Christmas present you've given me, that Tony should bring you home to us.'

Jenny felt vaguely discomforted by the older woman's words and manner. It suddenly struck her that Mrs Knight's previous questions formed the kind of quiz a mother might direct at a prospective daughter-in-law. If there was such a misconception it needed to be corrected. Fast. Before Jenny could sort out her dilemma a shout reverberated down the hallway.

'Hey, Tony!'

'Hey, Rob!'

Tony erupted from the studio, his answering yell ringing in their ears. Jenny glimpsed the beaming delight on his face as he bounded through the room to meet his brother. They collided in the doorway, virtually shaking each other, not content with mere hands. Wisecracks flew off their tongues in a bubbling stream, and the sheer joy of seeing each other again was in every word and gesture.

Jenny was fascinated by the startling contrast in their looks. She had expected Robert to be an older version of Tony but there was no similarity at all. He was not so tall nor as heavily built, and he was as dark as his brother was golden. Despite Tony's glowing tan, Robert's skin was darker and instead of a profusion of yellow-blond curls, his hair was shiny black with only enough wave in it to be fashionably shaped. He was nowhere near as handsome as Tony. His face seemed too angular with its high cheek-bones, lean cheeks and chisel chin, yet it was striking, somehow more distinctive than Tony's more classical mould.

Suddenly his gaze turned to Jenny and his eyes were riveting, not the dancing blue of a summer sea but large, dark, intelligent eyes which seemed to know too much. Her heart contracted as if it had been squeezed. Then in double-quick time it proceeded into a disturbing series of hop-step-and-jumps.

'Well, little brother, what do we have here?' he drawled with lazy interest.

Even his voice affected her physically, deep

vibrations finding chords of response. It was crazy, unreasonable to have such a reaction to a man. He was only Tony's brother. She tore her eyes from Robert and looked at Tony, needing to draw on the normality of her relationship with him.

'Little brother, hell!' he grinned, slapping Robert's shoulder in playful derision while sweeping his other arm towards Jenny. 'This is my landlady. And the emphasis, old son, is on the word lady. So behave accordingly. My goodwill depends on it.'

'Indeed!' One black eyebrow arched speculatively.

Jenny's skin crawled as every detail of her appearance was logged and assessed. She wished she had taken more care. The denim skirt and vest had seemed practical and tidy when she had chosen them this morning but now her outfit seemed drab and uninteresting. She probably looked like a schoolgirl with her long brown hair twisted into a single plait. And her face was sure to be shiny, showing up the freckles even more than usual. If only she had looked devastatingly pretty she might have attracted this man enough to retain his interest.

He turned to Tony. 'And may I know her name?'

'Jenny Ross. My brother, Robert E. Lee. His underlings call him The General. Silver-tongued like a Southern gentleman, but crafty and ruthless under the veneer, so be warned.'

'Cut the comedy, middle-man.' Robert's smile held a slow, confident charm as he came forward and offered his hand. 'A pleasure to meet a lady, though how you can be a friend of Tony's . . .'

'Watch it, brother!'

He threw a grin back at Tony. 'Well, you can hardly call yourself a gentleman.'

'I have the soul of a gentleman,' Tony retorted with offended dignity. 'You only have the veneer.'

Robert laughed. The fingers which closed around Jenny's were long and slender, their touch sensitive but strong. Although his stature was smaller than Tony's he was far from weak. There was a whipcord strength about him, fuelled by enormous reserves of intense energy. Jenny felt caught and enveloped in that energy, as if this man generated a force-field which was inescapable.

'A landlady?' he asked quizzically.

His thumb absently stroked her hand, projecting an intimacy which held Jenny in thrall. Somehow she forced her tongue to work. 'Only Tony's,' she got out, then blushed as she realised how very personal that sounded. 'I'm a music teacher,' she added even more stiffly and cursed herself for her inability to act naturally with him.

'And wait till you hear her sing, Rob. Jenny's my own private song-bird and she puts all yours in the shade,' Tony declared with possessive pride.

A shadow of reserve dimmed the brilliance of the dark eyes and the smile took on a cynical quirk. He dropped her hand. 'So, you're a singer.'

Her embarrassment deepened. She fiercely

wished that Tony had held his tongue. She felt
far too vulnerable to this man's opinion to ever
invite his criticism. 'No ... no,' she stammered
in denial. 'At least ... only for my own pleasure.
Not ... not in the kind of class you're used to.'

'Above it,' Tony boasted.

'Tony, please stop it,' she begged.

He gave an exaggerated sigh. 'She who must be
obeyed has spoken.' Then he grinned. 'All right,
Jenny-wren, but you'll prove me right before this
holiday's over. Rob shall have to concede.'

Robert was searching her face with such sharp
intensity that Jenny felt he was peeling off her
defensive layers, reaching for the inner most core
of her, giving her total concentration, as if she
alone existed for him in this moment of time. No
one had ever given that feeling. It was disturbing,
exciting, exhilarating.

'I think you'll find Jenny interesting, Robert,'
Annabel Knight remarked. 'I'm looking forward
to seeing her sing myself.'

'Seeing?' He flicked his mother a quizzical
look. 'Surely you mean hearing.'

'You can listen. I'll watch.'

'Ah!' He turned back to Jenny, his gaze more
speculative. He smiled and his smile was a polite
dismissal. 'Well, Jenny Ross, it would seem that
you can surprise me. Tonight?'

He swung towards his mother without waiting
for an answer. Jenny was conscious of a sharp
sense of anti-climax, as if some pulsing vitality
had slipped away before it had been caught or
defined. She felt strangely detached as the
conversation flowed around her.

'Miranda said to tell you she'd be home for

dinner. I hope to make it back here by eleven, if all goes well at the studio.'

'Got a programme, Rob?' Tony asked with a tinge of disappointment.

'The usual Christmas Eve show. Choirs and carols. I only dropped by to say hello. Long time no see, little brother.'

'Yeah. It's been a while. Great to see you again, Rob.'

'I'm free and clear after tonight. Plenty of time for us to get together over the holiday weekend.'

'What! No women on a string?' Tony scoffed.

'Very loosely. And look who's talking,' he drawled with a teasing look at Jenny.

She flushed and silently directed Tony to correct his brother.

Tony adopted an expression of holy innocence. 'I'll have you know we have a very pure relationship. Almost antiseptic.'

Robert laughed and slapped him on the shoulder. His eyes twinkled amusement at Jenny. 'If you can reform this character you're a woman in a million. And it's not only a pleasure but a privilege to meet you,' he declared fulsomely. 'But now I must go. I'll see you all later.'

'I'll walk out with you,' Tony said and matched action to words.

Their voices drifted back down the hallway until the front door cut them off. Jenny sighed as if she had been holding her breath for a long time.

Annabel Knight smiled at her. 'They're very fond of each other.'

'I know. Tony often speaks of Rob.'

Strange that in all the words Tony had spoken

she had never received a clear image of his brother, only snatches of his life which had failed to impart the essence of the man. Robert Knight was a dynamic person, sure of himself and sure of his power to dominate others. People would always be aware of him. He was a hawk, and hawks flew in much higher spheres than wrens. A little ache of hopelessness settled in Jenny's heart. She would be no match for him.

CHAPTER TWO

JENNY loved her room. It was so large and so delightfully old-fashioned with its four-poster bed, white lace pillowslips and bedspread. The furniture was unashamedly Victorian, beautifully kept and gleaming richly with years of polish. She had enthused over it to the housekeeper who had smiled with pleasure.

'Well, Miss Ross, this is one room I can do what I like with, and they are few and far between in this house, believe me. I can't sweep the studio when Mrs Knight is painting. I can't dust the study because Mr Knight doesn't want his papers and books moved. I'm only allowed to vacuum the floor and change the linen in Mr Robert's room and Miss Miranda insists on doing her own. When she gets around to it.'

The grumbling had all been good-natured. Tony had called Mrs Cherry an institution, having been with the family for as long as he could remember. A widow of long standing, she was now in her sixties, but still staunchly upright and clearly a fastidious woman who took pride in her position.

'All the same, it must be an interesting family to be with, Mrs Cherry,' Jenny had replied warmly.

'Eccentric! Every last one of them,' the housekeeper had sighed as if it was a cross she had to bear. 'And young Peter might very well be the worst. He's had the billiard room commandeered since the school holidays began. Thousands of tiny soldiers all lined up to do battle. And his father encouraging him. And he all of sixty. Second childhood, if you ask me, playing with toy soldiers. But they're all goodhearted. I'll say that for the Knight family. Good-hearted people,' she had repeated with the fondness of long familiarity.

Jenny had to agree. She mused over the afternoon's meetings as she brushed her hair. She was glad now that she had come. The whole family had welcomed her, making her feel at home with them, even the maligned Peter whose teenage awkwardness had found a ready sympathy in Jenny's heart. He lacked the easy charm of the adults but he had made a gallant effort to overcome his self-consciousness. The thin gangliness of youth and a slight acne problem made him something of an ugly duckling in the Knight family but his dark, shiny eyes held the same vital life as his oldest brother's.

Robert Knight. Just the thought of him brought an unaccustomed flutter to Jenny's stomach. Strange that he should make such a forceful impact on her in only a few minutes' acquaintance. She wished Tony had not burbled on about her singing. Robert Knight was probably used to being accosted by young hopefuls pushing for a break into the big-time. There had been that hint of suspicion in his eyes, a cynical tone in his questions. She hoped he had believed her answers. It would be awful if he thought she was using Tony's invitation to promote herself. She wanted him to notice her, but not from a professional viewpoint.

With the skill of long practice she twisted her long, straight hair into a tidy top-knot. The humidity of the evening made leaving it hanging around her neck an unattractive idea. Besides, the style lent her face a little dignity. Freckles inevitably gave her a childish appearance and tonight she very much wanted to look a mature adult. Robert had said he would be home at eleven o'clock. Anticipation tingled through her veins.

After careful deliberation Jenny chose the cool, green dress which always made her feel good. It was well-cut and fitted her perfectly. It even seemed to make her eyes look green instead of an indeterminate hazel. She told herself she was being silly. She simply did not have the equipment to attract a man who was mixing with beautiful women all the time. But common sense was a weak voice against the excited beat of her heart.

'Are you decent, Jenny?' Miranda's lilting voice called through the door.

'Yes. Come in.'

Jenny had found it difficult not to stare at Miranda when she had arrived home that afternoon, but Tony's sister had seemed completely unaffected by her own beauty. Her open friendliness was equally unaffected. She entered now in a swirl of wide-legged, lounging pyjamas. The cornflower blue of the soft crêpe material emphasised her beautiful eyes. Miranda exuded glamour from every luscious curve of her tall, Junoesque figure and Jenny could not quell a little stab of envy. While her own petite figure was undeniably feminine, it was nowhere near as eye-catching as Miranda's. She smothered a little sigh as the other girl flounced on to the bed and arranged herself comfortably.

'I've been dying to get you alone and pump you about Tony and I'm not going to move until you tell me all,' Miranda announced with gleeful anticipation.

'What about him?' Jenny asked innocently, sitting down to strap on a pair of high-heeled sandals.

'Don't you know you're the first girl he's brought home in his whole twenty-six years?'

'Truly?' The word was more surprised than question.

'Truly. And that, in case you don't know it, makes you someone very special.'

'I think you've got the wrong idea, Miranda,' Jenny said, looking up with a wry smile. 'We're just friends, you know. Tony felt sorry for me because it was Christmas and I have no family.'

'Oh yes,' Miranda agreed with arch disbelief.

'Believe it or not, I'm not part of his love-life. We just share the same house,' Jenny insisted.

'Uh-huh. All platonic, is it?'

'All platonic.'

'Well, that just goes to show how special you are.'

'How do you work that out?' Jenny mocked as she stood up to apply a soft-coral lipstick to her mouth.

'Because Tony is a born wolf. He's been gobbling up girls since he's been in his early teens. If he's leaving you alone he must respect you an awful lot.'

Jenny looked at Miranda's reflection in the mirror, silently comparing the perfect features and the sensuous fall of blonde, silky hair with her own undistinguished appearance. 'I'm not exactly a sex siren,' she remarked dryly.

'He watches you all the time. Don't tell me you're blind,' Miranda protested.

'Oh, he's fascinated by my funny face,' Jenny replied, pulling a derisive grimace. 'For some obscure reason it's an artist's dream. Or nightmare. I'm not sure which. Maybe it's the freckles. I imagine they'd be very hard to paint.'

'Stop putting yourself down. You have a lovely face. Has he painted you?'

'I haven't sat for him if that's what you mean. You're way off line, Miranda. Tony has other girls.'

'But you like him, don't you?'

'Yes, of course. Who wouldn't like Tony?'

'Love him?' Miranda persisted.

'Like a brother,' Jenny teased.

'Jenny Ross, I'll get you for that,' Miranda threatened darkly. 'There is more to this than you'll admit.'

Jenny laughed and shook her head. She put her lipstick away and turned around. 'Well, I'm ready.'

Miranda sighed. 'All right. But you can't keep a secret in this house, you know.' She slid off the bed, all her movements unconsciously graceful. In an endearing gesture of friendliness she linked her arm with Jenny's for the walk downstairs. 'Anyway, I'm glad you're here. With three smart-tongued brothers a girl needs some feminine support.'

Dinner was a lively affair with Tony and Miranda engaging each other in quick-witted repartee. They were so alike as to be almost twins. Their father, Edward Knight, kept provoking them into verbal battle with dry-humoured remarks, and even Peter came out of his shell to stir the mixture occasionally. Jenny enjoyed their company immensely, even to the extent of involving herself in the general gaiety.

Annabel Knight called them all to order whenever they became too boisterous but her eyes held a delighted twinkle. Jenny noticed the looks of intimate sharing which passed between wife and husband. It was obvious that here was a deep, abiding love and she could feel it winding around their children. It was indeed a happy household and the benign satisfaction on the housekeeper's face as she flitted to and fro emphasised the fact.

After dinner they all retired to the formal lounge where a huge Christmas tree took pride of place, glittering with a mass of tinsel, coloured lights and all the traditional decorations. Only a room of such spacious proportions could have housed such a tall, magnificent tree. The fragrant scent of pine-needles assailed Jenny's nostrils.

'Why, it's real!' she gasped.

Edward Knight chuckled at her look of wonder and delight. 'Annabel wouldn't have it any other way. Even now she has the heart of a child. Every year it's off to the markets to find the very best tree. It's almost a feat of engineering to set it up in here but we have to do it. Come, my dear. Sit with me while we have coffee. We need to be better acquainted.'

He steered Jenny to a sofa and saw her settled comfortably before lounging into its corner where he could observe her without having to turn his head. He had the lean, facial structure which his eldest son had inherited but he was heavier in build and fleshier around the jaw. His hair was white and thinning. The mellowness of age was in his manner but it was belied by eyes so dark as to be almost black, eyes which were lit by a very keen intelligence.

'Tell me what you think of my two extroverts,' he invited, nodding to where Tony and Miranda were engaging their mother in conversation. Peter sat quietly nearby, a superior smile of amusement twitching at his lips as he listened.

'They have the air of owning the world,' Jenny remarked, then added wryly, 'but the beautiful people do, don't they?'

Edward Knight shook his head. 'There's a natural arrogance which comes with beauty, a confidence in oneself which seems to bring an easier personal life. But for the very reason that life comes easier, they don't aspire to be owners.'

'Like Robert.'

The dark eyes sharpened. 'Very astute of you.' A pause, then, 'You were impressed by Robert?'

A self-conscious flush crept up Jenny's neck and her gaze wavered from Edward Knight's keen probe. 'It's just that he's so different from Tony. I was expecting them to be alike, but they're not,' she finished lamely.

'No, they're not,' came the soft agreement. 'The world was made for Tony's pleasure but

Robert has to hold it by the scruff of its neck. And he's succeeded in his field. The television shows he produces and directs have an extra touch of class. He's very much in demand and very much in command. Not only is he a meticulous organiser but he has a creative insight which can draw remarkable results.' His lips curled into a wry smile. 'Unfortunately that only applies to his professional life.'

The heavy sigh which punctuated the last comment drew Jenny's curiosity. She looked questioningly at Edward Knight, but hesitated over giving voice to words which might reveal too personal an interest.

The all-too-knowing eyes picked up the question. 'His personal life? That, my dear, is singularly barren, although Robert would probably not agree. The drawback to working among show-business artists is that most of them are looking out for number one. They're committed to their work and relationships tend to become a matter of convenience. The fact that Robert is still living at home speaks for itself. Only here does he feel a sense of permanence. It grieves me that he has become so cynical about people but I suppose I should be grateful that at least he still values our family life.'

His gaze drifted to his wife and his expression softened. 'What Robert needs is a close relationship with a good woman and he might just recover his humanity. The pity of it is, I'm not sure he'd recognise a good woman any more.'

Disappointment squeezed Jenny's heart. The little hope that she had been unable to repress seemed even more futile. If Robert was so very

cynical it was unlikely he would see any good in
her. She suddenly realised Edward Knight's gaze
had returned to her and it held a sharp
speculation which crawled under her skin. Had
he guessed what was on her mind?

'Are you very attached to Tony? Forgive me
for asking so directly but we haven't seen Tony
for six months and he is my son ... as well as his
mother's,' he added dryly.

Jenny smiled with relief. 'Mr Knight, I didn't
realise it was unusual for Tony to bring someone
home with him, but as hackneyed as it sounds, we
are just good friends. Tony did not want me to be
alone at Christmas-time because ... well, because ...'

'Annabel told me of your recent loss,' Edward
Knight cut in sympathetically. 'You must feel
very alone. I'm sorry.'

'It's not so bad now. Tony was a Godsend. He
cheers me up whenever I'm down in the dumps.'

Again came the knowing little smile. 'It's just
that he hates long faces.'

Jenny smiled back. 'You mean the sun must
always be shining for him.'

His mouth suddenly widened to an open grin
at her accurate perception. 'The light has to be
right. How else can he paint?'

They laughed and of one accord, looked at
Tony.

'And just what has my revered father been
saying about me?' he demanded, catching their
amused eyes on him.

'How very pleasant it is to see you,' his father
answered smoothly. 'Even if it did take Christmas
to bring you home on a visit.'

'Bearing gifts, Dad, to solace you in your venerable age. And what better gift than music for your soul? I'll get your guitar, Jenny.'

'Tony, no!' she protested quickly.

'It wouldn't be Christmas Eve without some carols,' his mother urged, unashamedly abetting her son who had ignored the protest anyway.

'In that case everyone will have to sing,' Jenny insisted, panicking at the thought of being spotlighted in front of this talented family.

'Not me,' Peter grinned. 'My voice is breaking.'

'No excuse is acceptable,' Jenny retorted determinedly. 'It's the spirit of the thing which counts.'

'She's right, Pete. No outs tonight,' his father declared.

In the end they all did sing, helped along by a considerable consumption of Christmas punch which Edward Knight had liberally doctored with alcohol. It was late in the evening when Jenny was finally prevailed upon to sing solo. It had been such a happy night she no longer felt quite so self-conscious about her voice and Robert had not arrived home as yet. The others were eager to enjoy her singing, however unprofessional it was.

Miranda requested 'The Little Drummer Boy' and Peter offered to provide the right sound effect by accompanying Jenny's guitar with his bongo drums. Free of the fear of being heard by really critical ears, Jenny sang without any other thought but to give the song all its depth of feeling.

There was dead silence when she finished. She

glanced up to see Robert Knight step into the room. For a moment their gaze locked. Jenny's heart seemed to hesitate, then resumed pumping at a faster rate as if to make up for the missed beat.

'Oh, hi, Rob!' Peter called out.

Then everyone was greeting him, drawing him into the family circle.

'Programme go off without a hitch?' his father asked.

'Smooth,' he nodded.

'We had our own programme,' Miranda declared smugly.

'So I heard as I came in.'

'Well?' Tony demanded.

'Well what?'

'You must have heard Jenny sing.'

Robert turned and smiled at her but the dark eyes held a guarded expression. 'You have a very sweet voice, Jenny. I enjoyed your rendition of the last verse. I'm afraid that's all I heard.'

Damned with faint praise, Jenny thought with dull resignation. Robert Knight was being tactful. She knew her voice was not commercial and she had not expected enthusiasm from him, but for one aching moment she savagely wished he had been impressed by her singing.

'Then you haven't heard her properly,' Tony insisted and gave Jenny a look of cocksure confidence. 'Give him another song. You'll show him.'

'Tony, I'm sure your brother has had enough carols for tonight,' she demurred in a firmly dismissive tone.

'Would you mind, Jenny?' Annabel Knight

asked sweetly. 'I would like Robert to see you perform. Come, sit here, Robert.'

She patted the chair next to hers and looked at Jenny expectantly as her eldest son complied with her wishes. A heavy reluctance dragged at Jenny's heart but she realised it would be churlish to refuse the request. She noted the air of long-suffering patience in Robert Knight's posture as he slumped into the chair. A little niggle of pride prompted her selection for this first and last audition.

'Since you give me little choice, Mrs Knight, I hope you won't mind if I choose one of my own compositions. My father was very fond of the early Australian ballads, even naming me after the girl in one of Henry Lawson's poems, "The fire at Ross's Farm". It makes a long song so please bear with me. I played it for Dad last Christmas and I'd like to play it again.'

Without waiting for comment Jenny played the first chord on the guitar and began singing. Her voice gave vibrant life to the story of the feud between the squatter, Black, whose illegally claimed land had been partly taken over by the farmer, Ross. Her tone softened as she told of the love which grew between Black's son and Ross's daughter, then quickened with urgency as the bushfire swept down and threatened the farmer's wheat crop on Christmas Eve. Robert Black's plea to his father to send help and the squatter's bitter refusal were played in sharp staccato, fading into weary inevitability as Robert and Ross fought alone in a vain effort to stop the flames. A quick crescendo ushered in the dramatic arrival of the squatter who had relented and brought his men to battle against the imminent disaster. The last four lines were delivered with quiet triumph.

> And when before the gallant band
> The beaten flames gave way,
> Two grimy hands in friendship joined
> And it was Christmas Day.

The last soft chord faded into silence. Jenny felt too choked to look up. A wave of grief accompanied the memory of her father's pleasure in the song. She did not see the look which passed between Edward Knight and his eldest son. It was Peter who broke the hushed silence.

'I say, Jenny. That was terrific!' he remarked enthusiastically.

'Thanks, Peter,' she smiled, blinking back the tears which threatened.

'Beautiful, just beautiful!' Tony breathed. 'Why haven't you sung it for me before, Jenny-wren?'

'I guess it was too personal,' she answered wryly.

Robert had not said a word. She flicked a quick look at him, anxious to know his reaction. His expression was one of bemusement but the slight shake of his head told her more clearly than words that she had failed. She had been a fool to think she could impress him, a man who worked with professional singers all the time. She knew her limitations, yet she felt doubly hurt by his silence. The song had meant so much to her and she had given it everything. It had still not been enough.

'Thank you, Jenny,' Edward Knight said with

soft sincerity. 'Your father must have appreciated your song very much. I know I did.'

The kind words brought a flood of self-conscious colour to her cheeks. 'Thank you, Mr Knight,' she muttered and bent over to put her guitar back in its case.

'Don't put it away. Sing some more,' Miranda urged.

'No, Miranda,' her mother intervened. 'We've imposed on Jenny's generosity enough for one night. Thank you, my dear. It was ... an experience. Robert?'

'Yes. Yes it was,' he murmured in vague agreement.

Jenny's cheeks burnt more fiercely. She did not want forced comments from Robert Knight. Tears stung her eyes. She could not bear any more politeness. She had to escape from the situation. Having zipped up the guitar case, she stood up and glanced around, not quite meeting anyone's eyes.

'Please excuse me. I'm very tired. I'll go up to my room if you don't mind.'

'Of course we don't mind, Jenny,' Annabel Knight said warmly. 'I hope you sleep well. We'll see you in the morning.'

Jenny nodded to the chorus of 'Good nights' and hurried away. It was a relief to reach her room and shut out the Knight family. They were positive, strong-minded people who made her feel insignificant in comparison. Not that she ever was anything but insignificant, she thought despondently, but right now she felt completely crushed into nothingness. Never before had she wanted so much to see appreciation in a man's eyes. And it had not eventuated.

She wandered around the room, listlessly putting a few things away in drawers. She felt restless but there was nothing to do but go to bed. With dull resignation she began to undress. As she hung the green frock in her wardrobe she thought it had not done anything for her tonight. A look in the mirror showed her lifeless, muddy eyes. She creamed the useless make-up off her face. Following her usual nightly ritual, she stripped off her underclothes and folded them neatly on a chair. She was completely naked when the knock came on her door.

'Jenny, it's me. Can I come in?'

She grabbed a cotton housecoat and quickly slipped her arms into it. 'What do you want, Tony?' she called back, reluctant to see anyone in her present mood.

'Oh, come on. What do you think I want?'

Jenny sighed. She was Tony's guest and he obviously wanted to talk to her. She wrapped the housecoat around her and tied the belt. 'All right. You can come in.'

He opened the door then hesitated, looking back.

'Not quite so tired after all, Tony,' came Robert's mocking voice from along the corridor.

'Barely tottering, old son. And good night to you too,' Tony retorted, stepping in and closing the door on Robert's soft laughter.

The blood drained from Jenny's face as she realised how their words must have sounded to him. Robert was not to know that Tony's visits to her bedroom had always been innocent. He had nursed her through influenza and there were few inhibitions left between them. Jenny was used to seeing Tony wander around the house with only a towel slung around his hips. The bathrobe he had on now was modest in comparison, but it must have been suggestive to Robert Knight. Their words would have seemed conclusive.

She felt sick. If there had ever been any chance for Robert Knight to become interested in her, that chance had been effectively nipped in the bud. She had just been firmly labelled in his mind as Tony's girl. Even worse. Tony's bed-mate.

CHAPTER THREE

'WHAT'S the matter? You've gone a bit green about the gills,' Tony remarked flippantly.

'You know what he thinks,' she snapped.

'So what? Rob's no prude. Good God! He's had so many women I bet he couldn't remember each one.'

'That's not the point. And you know it,' she accused with some asperity. 'I don't like your brother thinking that I'm sleeping with you.'

'All right.' He shrugged. 'I'll straighten him out in the morning if you're so fussed about it.'

'Will you?'

'Will I what?'

'Straighten it out,' she demanded impatiently.

'Yeah. Sure thing. I'll tell him you're a cast-iron virgin. That good enough?'

'Just tell him we're friends and nothing else,' she insisted with an uncharacteristic flash of temper.

Tony frowned. 'That's not like you. What's up?'

She threw up her hands in exasperation. 'Your whole family seems to have the impression that we're heading for the altar or something. It's embarrassing, Tony.'

He laughed, obviously having enjoyed the speculation he had aroused. He dropped on to her bed, stretching out in total relaxation before putting his hands behind his head and grinning at her. 'Come to think of it, it's not a bad idea. We have such a comfortable understanding. Why don't you marry me?'

She put her hands on her hips and looked at him with knowing mockery. 'And I ought to say yes, just to teach you a lesson, Tony Knight. You'd run so fast I wouldn't see the dust.'

'Nope. You're not getting rid of me that easily, Jenny-wren. I find our arrangement very cosy. No niggling demands. And besides, I'm very fond of you. You're a nice little song-bird and I like having you around.'

She sighed and sat on the bed next to him. 'It's worked out very well, hasn't it? You've been good for me, Tony.'

'Mmm . . . could be better,' he said with a glint of devilment in his eye. He reached out and curled a hand around her neck.

'Stop fooling! You know you don't fancy me.'

His hand moved upwards and he started pulling hairpins out. 'I could fancy you quite a lot if I received a bit of encouragement. Me . . . I never push. It's against my personal rules. But . . . if you ever have a change of mind . . .'

The intimacy purring from his voice jarred on her nerves. She looked sharply at him. 'Don't even think it, Tony. It'd spoil everything.'

'Would it?'

'You know damned well it would. What are you playing at, Tony? Has the change of scenery gone to your head? You think a bird in the hand will do because the two or three or four you usually have lurking in the bush, aren't here for your convenience?'

He removed his hand and put it back behind

his head, observing her through narrowed eyes. The fierce glare and flushed cheeks received thoughtful attention. Without a trace of humour he asked, 'Does my sex-life bug you, Jenny?'

A vague discontentment brought her to her feet. She strolled over to the dressing-table and picked up her hairbrush. Having dragged the rest of her hairpins out she began brushing hard. Tony's 'cast-iron virgin' crack had smarted. She replied to his reflected image in the mirror more curtly than she had intended. 'No, it doesn't bug me. At least you're honest. But when I go to bed with a man, Tony, I want to be the one and only woman in his life, crazy as that might sound to you.'

'You really are uptight,' he murmured. 'I'm sorry. I didn't mean to upset you.'

'You haven't. Not really,' she said dispiritedly. A wave of desolation swept over her as she stared at herself in the mirror. 'I wish I was beautiful. I wish I was so desirable that . . .' Tears sprang to her eyes. She choked them back and shook her head in mute distress.

'Hey!' It was a gentle protest. When she made no rejoinder Tony bounded off the bed and enveloped her in a warm bear-hug. 'You are beautiful, Jenny,' he insisted. 'I didn't realise just how beautiful you are until you were singing your song tonight.'

'That's only the artist in you speaking, Tony,' she sniffed disconsolately.

He tilted up her chin, forcing her to meet his eyes. 'As an artist I find your face an exciting challenge. It's as a man that I find you beautiful, Jenny-wren.'

She frowned and pushed away from him, discomforted by the unusual seriousness in Tony's manner. 'You're just saying that,' she muttered.

He sighed and lifted his hands in mock exasperation. 'What do I have to do to open your eyes? I'm not the only one, you know. Rob thinks you're beautiful too.'

Her heart gave a little flutter but the assertion was too unbelievable. 'Now I know you're lying.'

'I swear to you on a stack of imaginary bibles that I speak the absolute truth. After you left us tonight I asked him straight out. "Isn't she beautiful?" I said. His reply—and I'll point out that Rob chooses his words carefully when handing out an opinion—his exact words were, as I recall, "I have never seen anyone like her. Yes, she is . . . very beautiful." Ask Miranda if you don't believe me. She heard him.'

'He really said that?' Jenny asked incredulously. 'But . . .' She remembered his crushing silence after her song and shook her head. 'He was only agreeing with you, Tony.'

He glowered at her. 'You are the most frustrating, damned woman. Come here!'

He swept her into his arms and his mouth claimed hers before she had time to react negatively. It had been a long, long time since Jenny had been kissed and Tony was no gauche amateur in the art of lovemaking. Her inner restlessness responded to the persuasive skill of lips and hands which were telling her in no uncertain terms that she was desirable. It was not until she felt the hard probing of masculine desire that she was suddenly shocked back to her senses.

'No, Tony, no! My God what are you doing?' she cried in frightened protest.

Despite her frantically pushing hands he kept her lower body pinned to his. She had no defence against his strength. The haze of desire in the blue eyes slowly cleared. He smiled, a lazy, satisfied smile.

'Only what comes naturally, Jenny-wren.'

'Not with me!' she insisted, all too shamefully aware that she had been vulnerable to seduction.

One arm remained possessively around her waist as he lifted a hand and gently teased her lips with light fingertips. 'But you are very, very desirable, my little song-bird, and I wanted you to know that.'

His voice purred with sensuality, sending pinpricks of alarm over her skin. 'Please, Tony,' she begged. 'I don't want you to feel that way about me.'

One eyebrow rose in confident mockery. 'Don't you?'

'Oh, please stop it! I'm not one of your . . . one of your . . .'

'Don't you think I know that, Jenny?' he interrupted softly and his eyes were very serious.

'Then why? Why did you do that?' she demanded accusingly.

He touched her cheek in a tender salute. 'Because it was time you woke up.' A whimsical smile curved his lips. 'Call it a Christmas gift. Aren't we all supposed to be reborn at Christmas?'

She shook her head in bewilderment. 'I don't understand you, Tony. Please don't play games with me.'

'Stop worrying, Jenny-wren. Have I ever done anything to hurt you?'

'No,' she admitted shakily.

'Well, I don't intend to start now. You're safe with me,' he assured her. His face broke into a more Tony-like grin. 'So go to bed and dream sweet dreams, remembering that here's one man who thinks you're desirable.'

She stood there gaping after him as he made a jaunty exit from her room. For six months Tony had not touched her in anything but a friendly fashion. Now, suddenly, tonight he had introduced a sexual element, and she was not at all sure he had been fooling. His smile might have been whimsical but there had been nothing whimsical about his kiss. That had been very deliberately sensual, and his comment that she was desirable was more disturbing than comforting. She did not want Tony to see her as desirable. Only Robert.

It was frustration which had responded to his lovemaking. Much as she liked Tony she did not want him as a lover. Feeling slightly dazed by the switch in his manner Jenny pulled on her nightie, switched off the light and slipped into bed. She lay awake for a long time, trying to sort out her feelings about the two Knight brothers. Tony was like sunlight on water, bright, sparkling with good humour, fun to be with. He was not a shallow person but his attitude to life did not match hers. She needed the security he laughed at. She needed . . .

Her mind tried to grasp why Robert Knight attracted her so strongly. Was it the hard purpose she sensed in him? Perhaps she responded to a man who had that air of control and confidence. All she really knew was that she was affected physically and emotionally by his presence. And he had said she was beautiful. She nursed a pleasant little thread of hope as she drifted into sleep.

She rose on Christmas morning in buoyant spirits. The sun was shining and Robert would be at breakfast. She even had a specially pretty dress to wear. It was only a simply cut sundress but the white piqué cotton was liberally printed with sprays of cherries which gave it a Christmasy look. Red, cherry-shaped buttons ran from the low, heart-shaped neckline to the hem and she had bought a pop-art necklace which featured a small bunch of enamel cherries on a fine gold chain.

Carefully applied lipstick and a touch of green eyeshadow added colour to her face and Jenny brushed her hair until she fancied there were chestnut gleams among the brown. She practised a confident smile and hoped that Robert would think her beautiful this morning. Had he really said that? She shook her head in doubt, but the smile remained.

Unfortunately her confidence eroded with each step she took downstairs. She remembered Robert's soft mockery last night and hoped that Tony had explained his visit to her bedroom. A flush of self-consciousness warmed her cheeks as she followed the sound of brightly raised voices to the breakfast room.

The family greeted her warmly, Edward Knight's voice overriding the others. 'What a charming dress! My dear, you are the very spirit of Christmas. Come and sit by me.'

She slid into the chair on his right, too absurdly shy to look at Robert.

Tony was by the sideboard loading sausages and eggs on to a plate. 'You look good enough to eat, Jenny,' he declared, 'but I'll make do with these. What would you like? Bacon and eggs?'

'Yes, please.'

She glanced up at him gratefully, then let her eyes slide past Robert. He halted their casual traverse with a slow, appreciative smile. Her pulse leapt as though he had tugged it and she could not look away.

'Tony's right. A man could get an appetite for such delightful freshness. He's lucky to have a lovely landlady.'

The knowing tease in his voice deepened the flush on her cheeks. She squirmed between pleasure and embarrassment.

'Which reminds me . . .' Tony said in an attention-grabbing drawl. 'I have an announcement to make.'

The hushed expectancy around the table settled on Jenny as its focus. She threw Tony an agonised look of appeal. He answered it with a mischievous wink which only served to heighten the interest. Her appeal changed to a mutinous threat and he held up his hands in mock fear.

'All right! Don't get your feathers ruffled, Jenny-wren.' He glanced around the others with the smug air of having fooled everyone. 'Just thought I'd clear the air for Jenny who has found it thick with suggestions. Our relationship has not been a romantic one. And brother mine . . .' he cocked an eyebrow at Robert, '. . . she particularly did not care for the evil thoughts you entertained when you saw me going into her bedroom last night. When you share a house as Jenny and I do, bedrooms are not necessarily intimate places.'

'Is that so?' Robert's voice held an amused lilt but there was a cynical gleam in the dark eyes as he added, 'You have my apology, Jenny.'

Clearly he did not care if she had gone to bed with Tony or not. Her sigh was a mixture of disappointment and exasperation. 'Sometimes I could choke you, Tony.'

'See? I can't score with the woman at all,' he declared blithely. 'Last night she was taking me to task and now she wants to choke me. Just when I'm about to serve her with breakfast too. There's gratitude for you.'

'Thank you,' she muttered as he placed a plate of bacon and eggs in front of her and took the adjacent chair.

'Well, you should have told us,' Miranda scolded him. 'I'm sorry too, Jenny.'

'I'm innocent! I didn't think a thing,' Peter chimed in smugly. 'And what's more, you've just gone up in my estimation, Jenny. Only an idiot would fall for Tony.'

'I'll get you for that!' Tony threatened, pushing his chair back for action.

'Tony!' his mother warned sharply, then gave him an angelic smile. 'You can be Santa Claus this year and give out the presents from under the tree.'

'Blessed are the peacemakers,' Tony muttered with a grin at his mother.

Jenny tried to make peace with her stomach by eating a hearty breakfast and ignoring Robert as much as possible. Nevertheless she was doubly conscious of his voice and she could not help stealing an occasional glance at him. He looked so attractive in his casual, red-knit shirt and white jeans.

At last the meal was over and Annabel Knight gave the signal to rise. To her surprised delight Robert made a point of accompanying Jenny into the lounge. He took her arm and directed her to a two-seater settee, slightly apart from where the others settled.

'Since Tony is to do the honours around the Christmas tree and the rest of the family have enjoyed more of your company than I have, it's only fair that you sit by me,' he said with a smile which made nonsense of any sense Jenny had.

She sat next to him and was so terribly aware of his closeness that she had to force herself to breathe steadily. Rather than reveal the effect he had on her she directed her attention to the others until she could feel more at ease.

Tony was already hamming up his appointed role of Santa Claus, ho-ho-hoing with gusto as he eyed the pile of gifts and making a teasing business of selecting the first one.

'One for me,' Peter pleaded eagerly.

'You last, you slanderous-tongued monster, and a ho-ho-ho to you too.' Tony chortled evilly, then grinned at his mother. 'Mum comes first in this house.'

Although Jenny had bought small gifts for each member of the family she had not anticipated receiving any. To her surprise and delight, she was given a bottle of perfume from Miranda, a book by a popular cartoonist from Peter. Robert gave a record album. Annabel Knight's gift was an artistically patchworked cushion, and from Edward Knight came an old but beautifully produced book of *The Sentimental Bloke* by C. J. Dennis.

'It's not new, Jenny, but it's a collector's piece and I thought you'd like it,' he remarked as she leafed through it appreciatively.

'Thank you, Mr Knight. I'll treasure it always.'

He nodded contentedly.

'It's rare for my father to give away one of his books,' Robert murmured. 'You're honoured, Jenny.'

She glanced at him anxiously. 'Should I not accept it?'

His eyes regarded her with searching curiosity. 'He wouldn't have given it unless he wanted to. There must be more to you than meets the eye, Jenny Ross. I respect my father's judgment of people. I shall have to make a point of knowing you better.'

'I'd like to know you too.' Conscious of sounding too eager, she added, 'Tony's always speaking of you.'

'Ah yes. Tony,' he murmured. With a slight frown his gaze turned back to their appointed Santa Claus. 'At last he's come to his gifts.'

Jenny received a huge, pink panther sporting a wicked wink. 'To keep you company in bed,' Tony teased. Peter exclaimed delightedly over a book on the Napoleonic wars, and Miranda was given a screen-printed shawl. The two remaining gifts were obviously paintings. Tony presented the larger one to his parents. It was one of his latest landscapes and his mother enthused over it, much to Tony's pleasure. Finally he handed the last gift to Robert.

'I thought you needed this, Rob,' he said, a look of sheer devilment in his eyes. 'You see so many plastic ones, I figured you should be reminded that the genuine one exists.'

'Now you have me intrigued,' Robert retorted and tore impatiently at the Christmas wrapping. A second covering of brown paper held a white label. 'Portrait of a smile', he read aloud, then glanced up at Tony. 'A smile? Not your usual kind of thing, is it?'

'Take a look,' Tony grinned and gave Jenny a conspiratorial wink.

Robert ripped off the brown paper and Jenny gasped as she recognised herself. And yet it was not really her. Tony had interpreted her face differently to any image she had ever seen. There were barely any freckles and somehow she did look beautiful, caught in a moment of glowing pleasure. He had named it aptly. It was not a portrait of her but of a smile. She glanced up at him in sheer amazement.

'When?'

'I caught you the night you were playing the beach-party song to your pupils. I had other pencil sketches but that was the one I mostly worked from I haven't got the whole you but I did get the smile ... I think.' He turned to his mother. 'Want to look, Mum?'

'Dying to.' She quickly moved to behind the sofa and leaned over Robert's shoulder. 'It's good, Tony. Really good.'

'But not quite,' he sighed.

'Very close . . . for a difficult subject.'

'She drives me crazy . . .'

'I can imagine.'

'You shouldn't be wasting time on me,' Jenny protested, feeling embarrassed by their discussion of her.

'It's not wasting time,' he and his mother chorused, then laughed at each other.

'No. It's really something special, Tony,' Robert said appreciatively. 'Thank you very, very much. And I'll hang it in my bedroom so it'll be a constant reminder.'

'Good thinking! A smile a day keeps the psychiatrist at bay,' Tony chivvied him good-humouredly. 'Do you wonder that I like living with her?'

'Tony! I don't even look like that,' Jenny insisted.

He bent over and flicked a finger under her chin. 'Beauty, my girl, is in the eye of the beholder, and I've beheld you for six months. I know what I transferred to canvas.'

'You've been very sneaky.'

By this time the whole family had crowded around for a look.

'It's sort of like you, Jenny,' Peter proclaimed.

'Yes and no,' was Miranda's ambiguous comment.

'You've caught the essence,' Edward Knight said thoughtfully.

Robert looked up at his father who nodded. Then his gaze swept back to Jenny, alert and searching, a slight frown deepening the lines between the eyes. She suddenly realised that father and eldest son shared the same swift understanding which characterised the relationship between Tony and his mother. Robert's sudden and total concentration on her sparked a deep yearning for it to continue. She wanted to say, 'Yes, look at me and please keep looking', but lack of self-confidence made her own gaze waver and fall.

Annabel Knight invited discussion on Tony's landscape and the rest of the family moved to view it from different angles and air their opinions on its merits. Jenny had seen it before and Robert stayed at her side.

'You do look like this when you're singing, Jenny,' he commented.

She glanced down at the portrait in his hands and shook her head. 'I never look like that. For a start, Tony's missed out about a thousand freckles,' she said with light self-mockery.

'Is that how you think of yourself?'

'I don't have to think. I'm not blind. I see what's in front of me.'

He laughed. 'You call a spade a spade and a freckle a freckle. Is that it?'

'I've always considered self-deception pretty foolish.'

'It's equally foolish to underestimate yourself. The thing is to know what you've got and use it to your best advantage.'

She could feel the vibration of power from him. A little shiver ran over her skin. 'The killer-instinct,' she murmured, unsure in that moment if she was attracted or repelled. All she really knew was that she reacted to him. Strongly. Almost compellingly. 'Perhaps it's a question of defining what is the best advantage. Our views might differ on that, Robert,' she said thought-fully.

'If an opportunity is there to take, you take it, Jenny Ross.'

As he spoke he spread his hand, then clenched it into a possessive fist. The gesture seemed both exciting and frightening in its symbolism. She wondered how it would feel to be taken by Robert Knight. A primitive need stirred. She wanted to know. For the first time in her life, desire licked through her veins.

'Tell me,' he continued, 'have you composed any other songs besides the one you sang last night?'

'Oh, I fiddle around on the guitar.' She shrugged, suddenly shy under the sharp intensity of his gaze. 'It's just something I enjoy, you see.'

'How many?'

'A dozen or so, I guess,' she admitted, responding reluctantly to his demand.

'Would you sing them for me?'

She stared at him, startled by the request, yet excited by the interest he was showing in her. Her hands fluttered in helpless dismay. 'They're not . . . not polished . . . not like the one I did for my father. I worked hard on that because it was important. It was especially for him. The others . . . they've only been for my own amusement.'

He smiled. 'I'd still like to hear them.'

She flushed as a wild rush of elation danced through her veins. He really was interested in her . . . in her music, anyway. 'All right. I'll play them for you.'

'How about this afternoon? Lunch on Christmas Day usually runs late. Then everyone collapses with lethargy for a while, but four o'clock seems a good time.'

'Yes. Four o'clock then.' She did not care if he hated her songs. She would be spending time with him. They would talk. They would be together. Anything might happen.

'Oh, Rob,' Miranda called, interrupting the intimacy of their conversation. 'I was telling Tony last night but I forgot it when you came home. Dennis and Lorna Freeman asked us over for drinks this afternoon. Just a casual, drop-in affair between four and seven o'clock. We thought we'd go. You'll enjoy meeting them, Jenny. They're a way-out couple, but fun.'

Robert sighed and gave Jenny a wry smile. 'Well, that knocks our plans on the head.'

Jenny had a hard struggle hiding her disappointment.

'What plans?' Miranda asked.

'Jenny has a whole store of songs she's composed. I've just been persuading her to sing them for me.'

Tony had ambled over and he grinned triumphantly at Jenny. 'See? I told you he was impressed. Wait till you hear the beach-party song, Rob. That'll set your pulse going.'

'Apparently I'll have to wait since you're all off to a party this afternoon.'

'Aren't you coming with us?' Miranda demanded plaintively.

'I'm rather bored with that particular social scene. You can pass on my apologies.'

'Come on, Rob. It's Christmas,' Tony expostulated.

'Good will to all men?' Robert retorted

sardonically. 'Mine doesn't stretch that far. Particularly to all women. Lorna Freeman is not my idea of fun.'

'Uh-oh! Has she still got her eye on you?' Tony grinned.

'That woman leaves a rash, she clings so hard.'

'Poor Rob!' Tony commiserated mockingly. 'Well, the three of us will have to console Lorna for your absence.'

Jenny hesitated, torn between a sense of social obligation and her desire to stay with Robert. Then she spoke in a forced little rush. 'Tony, would you mind terribly much if I don't go with you? You know I'm not much good in a crowd of strangers, and Robert's interested in hearing my songs, and . . .'

'And you'd like to share your music,' he finished indulgently.

She nodded, her eyes pleading with him to make no protest.

Tony's smile held a wry twist. 'All right, Jenny-wren. Maybe Rob's opinion can give you some confidence in yourself.' The wryness became more pronounced. 'Though something tells me it might have been a mistake to introduce you to my brother.'

'How's that?' Robert drawled in dry challenge.

Tony cocked his head on one side, his eyes dancing provocatively. 'Let's face it, Rob. When it comes to the old physique, I've got you beat. But I suspect, only suspect, mind you, that you just might have a better ear than me.'

Robert laughed. Tony grinned. Jenny felt a flood of relief. It was settled. She was going to spend a couple of hours alone with Robert Knight.

CHAPTER FOUR

'I'LL get my guitar, shall I?'

Miranda and Tony had finally left for the Freeman's party and Jenny did not want to lose a minute of her time with Robert. Her whole body seemed to be bubbling with anticipation and it was difficult to repress the urge to run up the stairs like an over-excited child. She had already taken a few eager steps forward when Robert's voice halted her.

'Wait for me.'

She glanced back at him in surprise.

'Well go to my bedroom.'

The suggestion startled her. 'Your . . . bedroom?' she repeated hesitantly.

There was a sardonic quirk to his smile. 'I understood you had no objection to bedrooms as a place to talk . . . or sing. Or do you accord Tony privileges which are not to be extended to his brother?'

'I . . .' A painful flush was creeping into her cheeks and in a desperate attempt to gloss over her unease, she added quickly. 'All right. If you think that's the most suitable place.'

He grinned openly. 'Forgive me. I was tempted to see you blush again. I've turned my bedroom into a sound studio. It's the best place in the house for listening to music.'

'Oh.' It was a little sigh of relief.

His eyes twinkled with amusement as he drew

level and took her hand in his. 'It's also quiet and
private so we won't be disturbing anyone and no
one will disturb us. And I can listen to Miss
Jenny Ross to my heart's content.'

He started leading her upstairs. Jenny's arm
tingled with awareness as it brushed against his
and her cheeks burnt even more brightly at her
physical reaction to his closeness.

'Don't call me that,' she said shyly.

'What?'

'Miss Jenny Ross. It sounds silly.'

He laughed. 'It suits you. A woman who
blushes at the mention of bedrooms is an
anachronism in today's world.'

'That's a very cynical remark.'

'Possibly.' He threw her a teasing look.
'Perhaps I needed to meet someone like you to
make me less cynical.'

They had reached her bedroom and she darted
in to get her guitar, wishing fiercely that the
colour in her cheeks would cool. It was too
ridiculous to be acting like a gauche schoolgirl
when she wanted to impress a man of Robert
Knight's sophistication. She took a couple of
deep breaths to steady her pulse-rate before
rejoining him in the corridor.

He led her into a huge room. Except for the
presence of a large double-bed it could hardly be
called a bedroom. Banks of electronic equipment
lined one wall and there was a veritable library of
records, tapes and books. As for the bed itself,
Jenny had never seen anything like it. A curved
backpiece formed a semi-canopy which contained
reading-lights, shelves, an electronic clock-radio,
a small bar and a miniature television set. Only a

quilt and a pile of pillows showed it was also for sleeping.

Robert casually waved her towards a chair. 'I think you'll find that the most comfortable with your guitar.'

As she sat down he began threading a large reel onto a tape-recorder. A little chill ran through her nerves. A protest rose to her lips. 'Robert ...'

'Mmm?' He did not look around.

'You don't mean to ... Why are you doing that?'

He glanced at her questioningly. 'I'd like to record your music. You don't mind, do you?'

'But why? I told you ... please don't,' she finished limply, too agitated by the idea to express her feelings.

He swung around. Embarrassed by her emotional plea Jenny avoided his probing gaze.

'Why not?' he asked, obviously puzzled by her attitude.

Her mind searched frantically for words to explain. 'My ... my songs aren't professional, Robert. I told you that. You asked me to play them for you. Taping them makes it ...' Impersonal. She choked back the revealing word just in time and looked down at her guitar, feeling more and more wretched. This was not the kind of scene she had imagined with him at all.

He sat down in the swivel-chair near his equipment and leaned towards her. 'Jenny, music is my profession. The song you played last night had the touch of ...' he hesitated then continued in a more cautious tone, '... of something very special in its composition. If your other songs have the same touch, I'll want to listen to them more than once.'

She flicked him a wary glance. 'You said nothing last night.'

'You left rather abruptly. I was still evaluating what I'd heard.' His mouth curved into a slight smile. 'And I was somewhat bemused by your performance. I had just seen why my mother and Tony are so entranced with your face.'

She grimaced in irritation. 'I'm getting rather tired of hearing about my face. I can't find anything remarkable about it and my mirror certainly doesn't encourage me to keep looking.'

His smile grew wider. 'Your mirror won't show you, Jenny. You have an extraordinarily expressive face. Quite riveting when you sing as you did last night. In fact, you could very well be a star, performing in an intimate little club or restaurant where your face could be spotlighted. But that's what you'd need because your voice isn't strong enough to be commercial,' he warned kindly.

Her pleasure in his words brought warmth creeping back into her heart. Robert had liked her performance and he did not think she was altogether plain. 'I don't have any ambition to be a performer, Robert. I know my voice is thin and I guess I prefer to please myself with my music. Trying to sell it to others is not . . . I don't think I'm capable of it.'

'Do you mind pleasing me?'

'No,' she muttered with a quick downsweep of her lashes to hide how much she wanted to please him.

'Then let me record the sound of your music.

Just pretend the tape is not rolling. It won't be intrusive, I promise you, and it is important to me.'

He could not have said anything more persuasive. 'Well, I suppose you can always wipe it off,' she said with a resigned shrug.

He laughed as he swung around in his chair and flicked a switch. Then he was facing her again, satisfaction in his smile. 'I can almost guarantee that I shall have no wish to wipe it off. What was the name Tony mentioned this morning? The beach-party song? Shall we start with that one?'

'If you like.' Jenny leaned over the guitar, her fingers automatically reaching for the opening chord. The cherry necklace dangled distractingly. She put the guitar aside and reached up to take it off. 'It's in the way,' she explained as Robert raised his eyebrows.

His gaze travelled down her body, lingering on her breasts for a moment before dropping to her waist. 'Want to loosen your belt, too? Constrictions can get uncomfortable when you're singing.'

'No, it's all right,' she said hastily and picked up her guitar again. His brief appraisal had made her heart catch and now it was racing, drumming like a tom-tom.

Robert nodded encouragingly. Pride and a determination to please set her adrenalin flowing. The beach-party song was a lively tune, carrying a zing of excitement and a touch of devil-may-care. It suited her mood of the moment and Robert's rapt attention gave her the confidence to sing it well. When she had finished she looked to him for comment.

'Yes, it's there,' he said rather obscurely, but there was a gleam of excitement in his eyes. 'Another one?'

His insistent urging was all that Jenny needed. Already she had forgotten the silent rolling of the tape-recorder. She was playing to him. For him. 'I think of the next one as the wishing song.' It was a slower tempo, a more soulful and sentimental song. Jenny followed it up with a twangy tune of rebellion which she called, 'Not This Time'. She kept on with three more songs, varying the mixture so that no two held the same mood.

Robert's silence, his total concentration on her was very heady indeed. She felt they were in a closed little world of their own where emotion flowed between them to the swaying, soaring lilt of music. It was like being snapped out of a beautiful trance when he spoke.

'Enough for now. We'll have a drink.'

He leaned back and switched off the tape while Jenny put her guitar aside.

'What would you like?'

'What have you got?' she asked with a shrug.

He walked over to the bed and opened a small refrigerator which was camouflaged as a cupboard. 'Gin and tonic, Scotch and soda, orange or tomato juice if you'd rather keep off the alcohol. Just name it.'

'Gin and tonic, please,' she replied. It was not her usual drink but she did not want to give him the impression she was totally unsophisticated.

He handed her a long glass and nodded in a friendly fashion. 'Your songs are good, Jenny. A little unpolished, as you said, but they have an individual sound which grabs you.'

Her smile glowed with pleasure.

His gaze rested on her mouth, then slowly lifted, revealing a dangerous warmth before a dry mockery dispersed it. 'You want to watch that smile. It's enough to tempt a man into tasting it.'

Before she could think of a reply he had turned away from her, seating himself near the tape-recorder again. Jenny swallowed down half her drink, moistening a throat which was not dry from singing.

'So there's nothing between you and Tony,' he remarked off-handedly.

'It depends on what you mean by nothing. We're very good friends,' she answered as casually as she could.

'Doesn't seem like him somehow,' Robert muttered, absently eyeing his drink before sipping it.

'Tony's not really a wolf, you know. He only takes what's offered, and for a man of his looks, there's no lack of offers,' she said with a touch of irony.

'You don't mind? In your house, I mean,' he asked curiously.

'He doesn't bring his affairs home with him. Tony has a thing about that. He keeps his women quite separate from what he calls his real life.'

'And you're part of his real life.'

She shrugged. 'Well, I'm unavoidable in the house, but I keep right away from the toolshed which he's turned into a studio. That's strictly an invitation-only place and he doesn't invite very often.'

'What about you? Don't your men-friends look askance at your lodger?'

It was on the tip of her tongue to say she did not have any men-friends but she stopped herself just in time. She sipped her drink to cover the hesitation for thought. She did not want Robert to conclude that other men found her unattractive, and the truth was she had had no time for men before her father died. Afterwards she had been too depressed to start engaging in social life. And then Tony had come. He had given her companionship. It was only now that she felt the stirring need for something more than that.

'No one has objected to Tony's presence,' she answered evasively. 'We're not living in each other's pockets, you know. Sometimes I don't see him for days at a time. He'll go off in his van to sketch or paint somewhere, or virtually lock himself in the studio.'

Robert shook his head. 'Wonders will never cease.' A faintly derisive smile curved his mouth. 'Six months and not even temptation causing a ripple. Tony must be made of sterner stuff than I thought.'

His eyes were telling her that he would have found her a temptation under the same circumstances. Jenny squirmed inwardly at the suggestion. Although flattering, his attitude was flirtatious. She wanted him to be genuinely interested in her. She did not want to be considered as just another piece of flesh.

'Perhaps living in close familiarity takes the icing off the cake, so to speak. And I'm not exactly the continental kind, am I?' she said rather tartly.

'Continental cake can only be stomached in small doses. Shortbread I find palatable all the time,' was the smooth retort.

She raised a sceptical eyebrow. 'Am I supposed to feel complimented by that remark?'

He threw back his head and laughed. It was light, open laughter and there was no cynicism in his eyes when he spoke again. The warmth in his voice put a glow in her heart.

'I do like you, Jenny Ross. Most definitely. Ready to go on?'

Jenny nodded, set down her almost empty glass and picked up her guitar. The tape started rolling again. Robert did not move away. He sat watching her intently as she sang. Their closeness and his absorbed attention on her created an intimate mood between them. Jenny moved from song to song with barely a pause, and her introductory comment on each one was a communication to him, felt and silently acknowledged.

'That's all,' she finally sighed.

'You haven't done "The Fire at Ross's Farm".'

'That's so long. Do you want all of it?'

'All of it.'

Jenny finished what was left of her drink and settled herself again for this one last effort. It was a very personal song to her and emotion throbbed into her voice, making it richer in tone. When she came to the lines:

> And Robert fought the stubborn foe
> For love of Jenny Ross.

she could not resist the urge to see Robert Knight's expression. She lifted her gaze and a ripple of sheer exultation washed through her.

She faltered for a moment before picking up the next verse. The rest of the song was sung directly to him, all her energy directed towards feeding the hungry flame in his eyes. The last note died away. Without shifting his gaze from hers, he reached back and switched off the recorder. Jenny put her guitar aside as he stood, Then he was pulling her up into his arms.

Her lips were already parted in breathless anticipation. His mouth claimed hers in a long, searing kiss which swept away the memory of all the kisses Jenny had ever received. She responded instinctively, already aroused by the sexual awareness which had shimmered between them. His demands became more passionate and she gave whatever he asked with reckless fervour, her hands sliding around his neck, fingers thrusting into the dark thickness of his hair, blindly pressing for the chaos of sensations to find some resolution. His hands arched her against him, sliding purposefully down the curve of her spine, half-lifting her to fit her body to his in an intimate embrace which forcibly impressed his desire on her.

'Say yes,' he murmured against her lips, still tantalising them with touch.

'Yes,' she breathed.

His mouth caught her breath and stole it, intent now on total plunder. Jenny surrendered without reservation. He scooped her up and carried her over to the bed, laying her down and covering her body with his in one fluid movement. Her heart was palpitating wildly under his weight as he kissed her again and again until she was one heaving mass of emotion. Then he rolled to one side, pulling her with him but giving his hand room to undo the cherry buttons on her dress. His eyes held hers captive, promising pleasure as he murmured words of soft seduction.

'Your smile tastes sweeter than wine, intoxicating, as addictive as a drug. Undress me, sweet Jenny. I want to feel and taste all of you.'

She was intoxicated too, beyond anything she had ever imagined. The fever in her blood could not be denied. Her fingers fumbled with his shirt, clumsy in their haste to do his bidding. He quickly disposed of her dress and impatient with her slowness, he completed the task himself. In just a few heart-catching moments there was naked skin against skin and Jenny trembled with sudden apprehension at the unfamiliar intimacy of the contact, the soft yielding of her body to his hard masculinity.

'Not yet. Not yet,' he whispered huskily before taking her mouth again, this time exploring it with slow, deliberate sensuality.

Jenny felt as if she was spiralling down a whirlpool of sensation. Robert slid his body down over hers, his mouth trailing kisses down her throat, over the slight swell of her breasts, pausing to tease her nipples erect with his tongue, then moving lower.

Caressing hands persuaded her thighs apart. Jenny was melting, dissolving under waves of fierce pleasure. Every nerve-end seemed to be heaving with anticipation. She closed her eyes and swallowed hard but all control was slipping away. Her legs were trembling in little shivers and her breathing came in ragged gasps. Her hands clutched convulsively at Robert's shoulders.

He glanced up and saw the wild fear in her eyes. 'You don't like this?' he asked, moving up, warming her shivering body with his own.

'Yes . . . I do . . . I can't help . . . my reaction,' she answered jerkily.

'Not had many lovers, Jenny?' he murmured, brushing his lips across hers.

'I haven't had any,' she admitted, knowing he would soon discover that anyway.

His head lifted sharply. The dark eyes burned into hers, questioning and finding the answer. 'Oh God!' he groaned and rolled away from her, one arm shielding his eyes as he lay there, breathing heavily.

'Robert,' Jenny whispered anxiously, spreading a tentative hand on his heaving chest. 'I want you to make love to me. It doesn't make any difference, does it?'

His free hand came up and covered hers, squeezing it tightly. Then suddenly he threw it away and erupted off the bed. She watched in stunned disbelief as he grabbed at his clothes and dressed with sharp, angry movements. His accompanying words were even sharper, cutting Jenny to the quick.

'I wasn't making love to you. Don't you know that? Don't confuse me with the romantic Robert Black from your song. I was taking my pleasure from you. That's all. Physical pleasure.'

'No!' It was a moan of protest as her heart contracted into a ball of aching tension. Her body reacted instinctively, her legs drawing up as she bent double to absorb the pain of his brutal rejection.

He picked up her dress and tossed it near her feet. 'Put it on. You'll feel better,' he said grimly. Without another word he turned his back on her and walked over to the window. He stood there, stiff-backed and relentless, obviously waiting for her to comply with his command.

Sick with a hollow despair Jenny slid off the bed and dressed. She was doing up the last button when he wheeled around and spoke again.

'I'm sorry for the embarrassment I've caused. It never occurred to me that you were inexperienced.'

His tone was controlled, neutral. Jenny could not look at him.

'If I'd known I wouldn't have taken advantage of your high,' he continued.

'My what?' she asked, confused with an agony of emotion.

'Most performers are riding on a high at the end of a concert. It's virtually a sexual experience,' he stated matter-of-factly.

She stared at him in horror. 'You thought that of me? You thought . . .' It was too shaming, too contemptible. Tears swam into her eyes. Her hands fumbled with her belt, finally getting it through the buckle. She sat down and pulled on her sandals, her long hair curtaining the tears from his view. He had made her feel cheap and dirty and she doubted that she could ever look him in the face again. She stood up and made straight for the door, not bothering about her guitar. Her need to get away was too urgent. Once in her own bedroom she could cry out her misery in private.

A strong hand clamped on to her shoulder and spun her around.

'Don't go!'

'I want to.'

'No, wait!'

'What for? There's nothing for me here,' she cried in bitter protest.

'Jenny . . .' His other hand took hold and for a long, fraught moment his fingers kneaded the soft flesh around her shoulders. 'Jenny . . .' He sighed and his voice softened to a note of gentleness. 'Please listen to me.'

'You've said enough,' she choked out, keeping her lashes lowered to hide her distress.

'Please. I'd like you to understand. I've lived a different life to you. The people in it . . .' He drew in a sharp breath and let it out slowly. 'Sex is accepted as a . . . a passing pleasure. Sometimes just a release from tension, a nice way of winding down, given and taken without emotional strings. But it would have been wrong for me to take you like that. Don't you see? I couldn't. Not when . . .'. He was struggling to find the right words.

Jenny lifted her chin defiantly, pride demanding that she challenge him. 'I don't like people making my choices for me. I am an adult, twenty-three years old, and in control of my own life. I won't thank you for patronising me like a child.'

He frowned, uncertainty shading his eyes. 'Was it a conscious choice, Jenny, or were you simply swept along in the heat of the moment?'

He had made it impossible for her to admit what she had felt. The intimacy she had sensed with him had been a mirage, a figment of her imagination, a product of her own need reaching out and encompassing him. 'It doesn't matter now,' she said tightly. 'It was obviously a mistake. I'm sorry if you feel cheated of your pleasure.'

'Oh, hell and damnation!' he snarled. Then in an obvious attempt to regain control, he lifted a hand away from her and dragged it down his face. 'Look! I don't want to hurt you. I didn't mean you to be hurt. I guess I reacted a bit savagely. It was ... well, everything changed unexpectedly and ... dammit all! I wanted you.' He sighed and turned away, raking his hair with agitated fingers. 'You must think I'm an utter pig but ... I do have some shreds of decency. You don't take a woman's virginity just for idle pleasure. It should mean something.'

'I thought it did. More fool me,' she muttered derisively. Then before he could detain her again she was out of his room and running down the corridor. Her breath was coming in harsh sobs when she finally reached the sanctuary of her room. She shut the door and wished there was a bolt to secure it against any entry. She curled up on her bed and cried into the pillow, releasing all her desolation and frustration in a flood of tears until only an aching emptiness remained.

Knowing she would have to be present at dinner, she eventually dragged herself off the bed. With a little shiver of repulsion she discarded her Christmas dress, and hugging a housecoat around her she headed for the bathroom to have a shower. Tears fell again, mingling with the hard spray of water as she washed away the memory of Robert's touch on her body.

By the time she had briskly rubbed herself dry, Jenny had resolved that the only way to carry on within the family household was to pretend that nothing had happened. She returned to her bedroom and dressed in white slacks and a pretty crocheted top. She fastened her hair near her crown with a rubber band and plaited it into a coronet. Feeling fresher and tidier, she was composed enough to answer Tony's knock.

'Jenny? Are you awake?'

'Yes. Come in, Tony. I was just about to go downstairs. I guess dinner's almost ready,' she said in a bright rush as he came in with her guitar and cherry necklace.

'Rob said you had a headache.'

She shrugged. 'I had a long shower and I feel better now. Thanks for bringing my things back. How did your afternoon go?'

He gave her a lopsided smile. 'Oh, so-so. I'm not really wrapped in the plastic people.'

'Plastic?'

'Showy on the surface but no solidity. I like country people better. Rob was playing your tape through. Sounded great, Jenny. He's very impressed.'

'Is he?' she said tightly.

'Didn't he tell you?'

She made a conscious effort to relax. 'We didn't talk about them much. He did say I had an individual sound.'

He frowned. 'You sound a bit down.'

She forced a smile. 'No. I've enjoyed your family Christmas. Let's go down and join the others. Actually I feel like a drink.'

'A drink!' His brow cleared and his voice rang

with his usual cheerfulness. 'I had to drink like a
fish to dilute the quality of the company I've just
suffered. Maybe I can persuade Dad to open a
really good bottle of wine for dinner. After all, it
is Christmas.'

'Yes. By all means, let us be merry,' she
agreed. Because tomorrow I might very well die,
she added dismally to herself.

CHAPTER FIVE

IT was a tremendous relief to finally take her place at the oval table in the dining-room. Tony was on her right, Edward Knight on her left, Peter across from her and then Miranda. Robert Knight sat between Miranda and his mother, almost at the other end of the table and certainly too far away for conversation to be expected between him and Jenny. She had stayed glued to Tony's side during the pre-dinner drinks in the lounge. Following up his fiction of her headache, Robert had made a point of asking her if she was all right. Jenny had nodded, unable to bring herself to speak naturally to him. He had moved away and she had studiously ignored him.

Miranda dominated the table-talk for a while, giving an amusing report of the party she and Tony had attended. While she enthused about people and their doings Tony made humorous cracks about them, stirring his sister along. Edward Knight enjoyed their banter, his eyes occasionally twinkling at Jenny in shared acknowledgment of a particularly witty remark.

'Well, Peter,' he broke in as Miranda wound down. 'How have you filled in the afternoon?'

'I've been reading the book Tony gave me. And you know what I think, Dad? Napoleon was a fool to get mixed up with women. All through history the women of great men have been treacherous.'

'Power corrupts. It's the ultimate temptation. But I might add that the great men didn't treat their women too kindly either,' his father said dryly. Then with a loving look to his wife, added, 'And let me tell you, Peter, a good woman is everything. I dare say that if I lost your mother I'd go through the motions of living, but life would be very empty indeed.'

Jenny glanced up with a smile at Annabel Knight and caught Robert's eyes on her. She resisted her first impulse to look away and stared back at him, defiantly telling herself she had nothing to be ashamed of. She had given herself out of genuine feeling for him. His brutal rejection had tarnished that feeling but it still held her heart captive.

'How did you enjoy your afternoon, Jenny?'

She glanced sharply at Edward Knight, conscious that he might have intercepted that look between her and Robert. His expression was bland, his eyes merely interested.

'I understand Robert persuaded you into playing your other compositions for him,' he continued.

'Yes, I played them,' she answered briefly, not trusting herself to say any more.

There was a waiting pause. Jenny concentrated on her meal, pretending she was unaware of it.

'Robert?' There was a subtly critical note in the enquiry as if he was demanding to know what went wrong and why.

Jenny held her breath.

'Yes.' The word was not a question but an answer, firm and conclusive.

'Well?' his father persisted.

'I haven't had time to discuss it with Jenny, Dad,' he said quietly.

'Discuss what?' Miranda asked curiously. 'Honestly! You and Dad are as bad as Mum and Tony. This talking in shorthand drives me up the wall. Besides, it's positively rude at the dinner-table, isn't it, Jenny? Makes us feel all left out and ignorant.'

Jenny gave a faint, commiserating smile but made no comment. She wanted the conversation diverted away from her.

Miranda rounded on her brother. 'Well? Out with it! Explain yourself!'

Jenny could feel Robert's eyes boring into her but she did not look up. Again there was an excruciating pause. Then Robert spoke with quiet authority.

'Jenny has almost a unique flair for composing. It's not only the actual music, but the way it harmonises with the lyrics. The music interprets the words, giving them greater impact. It's a rare talent.'

She looked up then, unable to believe the opinion could be sincere. It was surely a sop to her pride. She knew and he knew there were faults in the songs. Her eyes rejected the consolation of his flattery. His steady gaze denied her silent accusation.

'Of course! You're right!' Annabel Knight burst out excitedly. 'That's why "The Fire at Ross's Farm" was so moving. The music expressed the whole story. How clever of you, Robert! I was so interested in watching Jenny I didn't appreciate the subtleties of composition.'

'Well, I mightn't have your keen ear, Rob,

but I always knew Jenny's music was special,' Tony declared triumphantly. He turned to Jenny with a delighted smile. 'Now maybe you'll believe me, Jenny-wren. The expert has spoken.'

'Yeah! I remember,' Peter chimed in. 'When the squatter and his men came on the horses, you could hear it in the beat. I say, Jenny? That's really clever!'

'Now, we've got to hear more of your songs. How about singing for all of us after dinner, Jenny,' Miranda urged.

'No!'

The biting negative swept out on a wave of panic before Jenny could snatch it back. Every pair of eyes around the table turned to her in surprise. All except Robert's, whose look of compassion caused her soul to writhe.

'I think Jenny's done enough singing for today, Miranda. She played twelve songs for me, and a performance of that length is physically and emotionally draining,' he stated, again with quiet authority.

His father supported him. 'Robert's right. It's too much to ask.'

Jenny almost sagged with relief. She was off a hook which had promised too much pain.

'However, you'd have no objection if we listened to the tape,' Edward Knight suggested pleasantly.

Jenny's heart stopped. Horror froze her veins. She had forgotten the tape. The tape which would have faithfully recorded all the emotion she had poured into those songs. For Robert Knight. Oh God! No! her brain screamed. She

turned to Edward Knight, her eyes begging him
to revoke the request.

'Please . . . I'd rather not. I didn't want Robert
to tape the songs. They're not . . . they're
not . . .'

'What Jenny is trying to say, Dad, is that the
songs aren't quite to the same standard of "The
Fire at Ross's Farm",' Robert cut in smoothly.
'She did not bother putting the same effort into
composing them. For her they were just an
enjoyable pastime, something she picked up now
and then, played with for a while, then tried
something else as the mood took her. Some of
them stand on their own merit but others lack the
final polish. The talent is undoubtedly there, but
not fully developed.'

It was a glib explanation which covered her
distress, and she was grateful for it. It gave her
a breathing space to recover her composure.

'Well, I've heard all of Jenny's songs and I
think they're fantastic just as they are,' Tony
boasted for her.

She could have killed him. She gritted her
teeth as he blithely continued.

'Rob's a perfectionist and Jenny invariably
thinks she's no good at anything, but I bet the
tape will knock you all out. Play it for us after
dinner, Rob. I want the whole family to hear just
how great she is.'

'I think the decision is Jenny's, not yours,
Tony,' Robert said firmly.

She could kill them both. She threw a dagger-
like glance at Robert. So now he was letting her
make a decision. Some decision! It placed her fair
and square on the spot.

'I would very much like to hear the tape, Jenny,' Edward Knight said with obvious sincerity.

'Me too,' Peter said emphatically.

'Come on, Jenny. Do say yes,' Miranda chimed in.

'We enjoyed your song so much last night, dear. We're all eager to hear more,' Annabel Knight added persuasively.

She felt like a trapped animal. There was no objection she could make which would not sound mean and ungracious. She was cornered. 'Very well,' she sighed. 'But don't blame me if you have a boring evening.'

'Thank you, my dear,' Annabel Knight said warmly. 'I'm sure you needn't fear that.'

What little appetite Jenny had found was irretrievably lost. She toyed with her food for the rest of the meal. The wine she downed with no trouble at all. She wished she could anaesthetise herself with it. Conversation drifted around several topics. She made a few perfunctory comments so as not to appear too silent. Her mind was testing out various escape routes because the evening ahead of her loomed as intolerable. A headache would be too obvious and she could not suddenly plead illness. It would be too rude to absent herself on any other pretext. In the end she resigned herself to suffering through the tape. Somehow she would have to pretend it was of no consequence to her.

The dominant position of the Christmas tree in the lounge more or less forced the family into a conversation group at one end of the room. Jenny could not escape the communal closeness. There

was no privacy for her and she was grateful that
Tony had sat down next to her on one of the
sofas.

The tree almost hid the huge, stone fireplace
behind it. On either side of it, polished cedar
cupboards reached almost to the ceiling. When
Robert opened them to reveal an elaborate hi-fi
system, Jenny realised there were built-in
speakers in each corner. They had been subtly
blended in with the cupboards. Her inner tension
grew as Robert threaded the tape on to a
machine.

'Relax,' Tony murmured. 'You're not on trial.
Besides, I love your songs. You know that.'

She gave him a wry grimace. 'They'll probably
sound awful on tape.'

'Well, you can't call Rob prejudiced and he
liked them.'

Her voice suddenly came out of the speakers,
loud and clear. 'Tony calls this the beach-party
song. I haven't given them formal names.'

She winced at the eager note which was plain
for all to hear. With firmly gritted teeth, Jenny
set her mind to building a strong, defensive wall
between herself and the Knight family. The tape
played on, uninterrupted until Robert's voice
came over declaring, 'Enough for now. We'll
have a drink.'

'Good thinking!' Tony called out with a grin.

'Yes. I believe champagne is definitely indi-
cated,' Edward Knight declared, getting to his
feet as Robert switched off the player.

'I say, Jenny,' Peter said admiringly, 'All my
friends would freak out over "Not This Time".
It's unreal!'

'And the beach-party one has a terrific beat,' Miranda added with bubbling enthusiasm.

'I like "Wishing" best,' Annabel Knight stated firmly. 'Only somehow it just misses out on being truly haunting. I think if there was a bit more contrast in the highs and lows of the melody, just slightly more drift to the sound, it would catch at your heart more.'

'Yes. That's what it needs,' Robert agreed.

'The lyrics are absolutely great, Jenny,' Miranda enthused. 'I'm good at memorising words but I couldn't string them together like that in a million years. If I had your talent, oh boy! What I wouldn't do with it!'

'You do all right, little sister,' Tony drawled.

Edward Knight returned with a bottle of champagne. 'Glasses, Annabel.'

His wife quickly moved to an elegant cabinet and produced seven beautiful flute glasses in elaborately carved crystal. 'We'll have the best,' she said with a special smile at Jenny.

Edward Knight made a ceremony of popping the cork and pouring out the champagne. 'Well, Jenny,' he said as he handed her the first glass, 'from what I've heard so far, all I can say is I'd like to toast a very wonderful talent.' He passed the champagne around and then lifted his glass to her. 'I hope we can persuade you to share it with everyone. There are too few people who can give pleasure.' He turned and nodded to his eldest son. 'Let's hear the rest of the tape, Robert.'

Jenny was surprised and deeply gratified by the avid interest on the faces around her. All the Knights had seemed genuinely impressed by what they had heard. Maybe her songs were as good as Robert had declared. Her gaze was inexorably drawn to him. He sat apart from the others, closer to the hi-fi equipment. He had his elbows on his knees, head lowered as if he was contemplating the carpet at his feet. She wished ... Jenny put a sharp clamp on the wish. Indulging in pipe-dreams was stupid. She was about to look away when he glanced up and caught her eye.

'That's all,' her voice sighed through the speakers.

Robert abruptly stood and switched off the tape. The dark brooding on his face suggested that he no more wished to hear the last song than she did. In the silence which followed Jenny wondered exactly how he felt now, what emotion lay behind that dark brooding. Then Peter stirred from his sprawled position on the carpet.

'Why didn't you do "The Fire At Ross's Farm"? I've been waiting for it,' he complained.

'You heard it last night,' Robert answered for her.

'But I want to hear it again. It was great!' Peter insisted.

'Surely you taped it, Robert,' his father remarked questioningly. 'The music was too good to miss.'

'Yes, I taped it,' he admitted tonelessly.

'Well, let's hear it,' Peter demanded.

'Peter, I was considering Jenny's feelings. After all, she did write it for her father last Christmas,' Robert explained quietly.

'Oh! I forgot,' Peter mumbled and turned to Jenny apologetically. 'But you did play it for us last night.'

'You can hear it if you want to,' Jenny replied, forestalling any further comments.

Her eyes defied Robert to make something of it. He gave a little shrug and flicked the switch which set the tape rolling again. It took considerable discipline to sit there and show no sign of her own private agony as the poem drew to its end. She fiercely hoped that no one could hear the vibration of need and desire in her voice. At last it was over.

'I don't think I've ever heard you sing with such feeling, Jenny-wren,' Tony commented softly. 'That was absolutely beautiful.'

'Yes. Beautiful,' his mother echoed and surprisingly there were tears in her eyes. 'What a wonderful Christmas gift for your father. He must have been so pleased and proud of you.'

'Thank you, Mrs Knight,' Jenny murmured. She had to blink rapidly to stem her own tears. The strain of the last few minutes had made her composure very brittle.

'But you really must work on the "Wishing" song. That has such wonderful promise. The lyrics are beautiful and the music almost lives up to them.' She looked brightly at her eldest son. 'You could help her, Robert.'

'No. Really, Mrs Knight. I . . . I can do it on my own,' Jenny stammered, in a rush to divert the imminent embarrassment.

'But an outside point of view can sometimes give you an insight which you miss by yourself,' she explained eagerly. 'And Robert's always been so good at constructive criticism.'

A hot tide of blood was creeping up Jenny's neck. She told herself severely to keep a cool head. 'Mrs Knight, you've been very kind. You've all been kind, and I'm glad you liked my music, but let's leave it at that. Please?'

'Jenny ...' Tony began with gentle persistance.

'No, Tony,' she cut in sharply. She had had enough of being pushed into a corner through courtesy, and she was certainly not going to be pushed on to Robert. 'It's my music. You wanted your family to hear it. Now they have. You're all very strong-willed people, but I ... I have a mind of my own too, and ...'

'And we've been very selfish,' Edward Knight said with soft apology.

'Oh no, Mr Knight,' Jenny retorted anxiously. 'You've been very generous with your praise.'

'But your music is very personal to you.'

'Yes,' she sighed, relieved that he understood.

'Then I can only say thank you very much for sharing it with us ... and forgive us our trespasses.' He smiled, taking all the tension out of the moment. Then in a very deliberate move he reached over and took his wife's hand, winding their fingers into a shared grip. 'Annabel, do you remember ...'

'Uh-oh!' Peter sighed in exaggerated melancholy. 'Here we go again with that old stuff. Give it a rest, Dad.'

His father eyed him sternly. 'Do I hear a note of disrespect, you young termite?'

'Termite!' Peter scoffed.

'You have the temerity to attack the foundations of my youth. I happen to be very fond of my memories.'

'Don't we know it!' Peter retorted cheekily.

'Off to bed if you can't be civilised,' his father threatened.

Peter put on a long-suffering face. 'I'm civilised.'

Edward Knight began a stream of nostalgia which was quickly swelled by his wife and children, remembering and retelling incidents from their childhood. Jenny enjoyed listening. Their stories distracted her from more personal thoughts and not having experienced a normal family life herself, she found the conversation fascinating and revealing. She discovered that Robert was thirty, six years older than Tony who was two years older than Miranda.

'I was the accident,' Peter declared with a grimace.

'Some accident!' Tony guffawed. 'You've been spoiled rotten. It's Rob I feel sorry for. After being the one and only he then had to cope with us two getting into his toys and books. And being told to look after us. Sometimes you must have hated us, Rob.'

'Resented you certainly. You were both monsters and you'd look all angelic and innocent if I complained. I used to think it was grossly unfair that you had blonde curls and big, blue eyes. You got away with murder and I was landed with the responsibility.'

'It was your own fault, Robert,' his mother chided, amused by his claim. 'You used to protect them from their misdeeds, deliberately shouldering the blame.'

'Oh well,' he shrugged. 'They were only little kids, and Dad sure packed a wallop when he got mad at us.'

Jenny wondered about that protective streak in him. Maybe Robert had thought he was protecting her this afternoon. She inwardly writhed at the memory of his rejection. She had not wanted his protection. She had wanted him to be so emotionally involved that rejection would have been impossible. A heavy sadness settled on her heart. She was glad when Tony started yawning and his mother declared it was bedtime. There was a general stirring of bodies and an exchange of goodnights. Jenny was on her feet, about to accompany Tony upstairs when Robert spoke in front of all of them.

'Jenny, could I have a word with you before you go?'

He had moved away and was rewinding the tape. She hesitated, reluctant to be alone with him yet impelled to hear what he had to say. Tony frowned at Robert, then raised questioning eyebrows at her. Jenny shrugged and after a moment, he shrugged also. With a wry little goodnight salute he trailed off after the others and left her alone with Robert.

He was in no hurry to speak. Slowly and carefully he lifted the tape from the player and placed it in its cover. Jenny suspected that he was waiting for everyone to be out of earshot. She tensed as he walked towards her. He stopped an arm's length from her and raised eyes which were dark with torment.

'I've been trying to think of what to say to you but every word seems hopelessly inadequate. You offered me two gifts this afternoon and I took them without appreciating the value of either. To say I've been a blind fool doesn't make my actions any more forgivable.'

He looked down at the tape in his hands. Jenny saw a muscle contract in his cheek. She made no reply. The tight constriction in her throat made speech impossible.

'I don't think I've ever admired anyone as much as I've admired you tonight.' His gaze swept up again and the taut strain in his voice was accompanied by a look of pained apology. 'You handled, with magnificent dignity, what must have been for you a very difficult situation. When I spoke of your music at dinner, I wanted to give you the pride you should have in your songs. And I thought the reaction of the rest of the family might help salve the hurt I'd given you.'

He sighed and his mouth curled in self-contempt. 'I was wrong. Just as wrong as I was this afternoon. I can't undo what I've done. I can only give your music back to you. I had no right to take it . . . or anything else.' He offered her the reel of tape.

Her fingers stiffly closed around it. Her heart felt squeezed with a conflict of emotions. The soft caring in Robert's voice was ripping away the defences she had erected, and a thousand needs were clamouring out for her to retain this man's interest, whatever the cost. 'Did you . . . did you really think what you said at dinner?' she forced out shakily.

'I would not have said it otherwise. There's magic in your music, Jenny, I only wish . . .'

She glanced up, anxious for him to continue. There was a deep yearning in his eyes which soothed some of the hurt he had inflicted.

'. . . I wish it was still possible for you to share it with me.'

'What . . . what do you mean?' she asked warily.

'I think you would derive a deep, personal pleasure from hearing the difference in some of your songs if you were to make a few adjustments, a different key, a change of phrasing here and there. I would've liked to have gone over them with you, helped you lift them to what they could be. But . . . I understand that . . .'

'I'd like that too.'

Her surrender sparked a flash of triumph before the warm glow of satisfaction settled in his eyes. 'Thank you,' he breathed softly.

Her lashes fluttered down to hide her uncertainty as Jenny thought about that odd reaction from him. 'I hope you mean what you say, Robert,' she muttered. 'I'd rather you back off now than play me along for the sake of . . . of making me feel better.'

'Jenny . . .'

She saw his hand lift towards her and she flinched away. Her eyes flared up at him, wounded and intensely vulnerable.

'Don't look like that! God in heaven! I didn't mean . . .' He swallowed and his hand carried up to his face, fingers and thumb squeezing eyelids together as if trying to wipe away the image which had pained him. 'Jenny, I assure you that I'm completely sincere.' Then he was gesturing a plea for belief. 'We'll work down here if you like. Anywhere you say.'

She expelled the breath she had been holding and some of her tension eased. 'No. That would

be silly. To achieve what you're talking about we
need to listen to the tape and re-record variations
until we're satisfied.'

'Yes, we do,' he agreed quickly. 'Have you
anything planned for tomorrow morning?'

'No. At least Tony hasn't spoken of anything,'
she added cautiously.

'Are Tony's wants more important than
yours?'

She flicked him a look of reproof. 'I am his
guest, Robert. I wouldn't be here at all, but for
Tony's kind invitation.'

'Yes, of course,' he muttered. 'Well then, if
Tony has no objection, shall we make a start in
the morning?'

'All right.' She glanced down at the reel in her
hand. 'You might as well keep this. It can be a
working tape.'

'Thank you. And I do mean that, Jenny.
Thank you very much.'

She gave him a guarded little smile. 'Well, I'll
see you in the morning. Goodnight, Robert.'

His answering smile was full of warmth.
'Goodnight, Jenny.'

Her treacherous heart gave a delighted skip,
belying all the dicates of caution and common
sense. She quickly turned away and hurried up to
her bedroom, hoping that tomorrow might clear
some of her emotional confusion. Robert Knight
was an enigma to her but he could not remain an
enigma if they were to work closely together.

CHAPTER SIX

JENNY'S stomach held too many flutters for her to enjoy breakfast the next morning. Conversation flowed around her but she remained silent, nervously aware of Robert Knight and wondering if she had been a fool last night. How on earth was she going to work in his bedroom and pretend that there was only music between them? How was she even going to work with her mind occupied with him?

Miranda was the first to rise from the table. She stretched with the sinuous grace of a cat and smiled at Jenny. 'I'm going to spend the whole day lazing by the pool. How about joining me?'

'Jenny's working with me this morning,' Robert stated flatly.

'Hey, come on, Rob! Fair go!' Tony immediately protested.

Robert raised his eyebrows in casual challenge. 'Fair go at what? I asked Jenny if she'd like to go over her music and . . .'

'It's a holiday, dammit! I brought Jenny home with me because she needed a break. Yesterday afternoon was okay. I wanted you to tell her how good her music was, because coming from you she'd believe it. And last night proved it to her. But there's more to life than music, big brother, and I mean to see that Jenny has some fun.'

'Maybe Jenny thinks music is fun, Tony,' Edward Knight remarked in a quiet, measured tone. 'Don't press your guest into what you want to do.'

'Now just a minute, Dad . . .'

'I think you should ask her instead of . . .'

'She accepted my invitation,' Robert insisted, overriding both Tony and his father.

They were doing it to her again, talking over her head and trapping her into an ambivalent situation where she would be hamstrung into making a decision she didn't want to make. To her vast relief, Annabel Knight intervened.

'Tony, I'm sure Jenny will enjoy working on her songs and there are some new techniques you've used in your landscape that I'd like to discuss with you. Perhaps you wouldn't mind spending the morning with me.'

There was a moment of tension when Jenny thought he was going to refuse. Then he collapsed back in his chair and lifted his hands in resignation.

'All right. Be glad to, Mum. Only you're not to keep Jenny locked up all day, Rob. I know you when you get your teeth into something. Time means nothing to you.'

'Like you when you're painting,' his brother retorted dryly.

Tony laughed and the last bit of friction evaporated. 'I warn you. I expect to see her at lunch.'

Robert smiled. 'I like to eat too, little brother.' His gaze swept to Jenny, warmly inviting. 'Ready to start?'

She hesitated, her nerves tightening as yesterday's scene in his bedroom sliced into her mind.

Edward Knight leaned over and patted her hand. 'I'm delighted that you listened to Robert's persuasion. Yours is a talent worth developing, my dear. I hope you have a very fruitful morning.'

'Thank you,' Jenny murmured and rose from her chair.

The morning had been arranged and the simplest course was to go along with the set arrangements. Everything seemed beyond her control in this household and her position as guest made resisting the dominant forces around her even more difficult. The Knight family seemed to regard her as a passive pawn to be pushed around at will . . . their will.

'You know I only agreed to this morning if Tony didn't mind,' she burst out resentfully as she accompanied Robert upstairs.

He hesitated for a moment, glanced sharply at her, then kept on walking. 'This is more important.'

His answer rasped over the wounds he had inflicted yesterday. 'What right have you to make that decision for me?'

They had reached the top of the stairs. Robert turned, dark eyes sweeping her with concern. 'I'm sorry, Jenny. Do you want to go back down?'

The abrupt change from arrogance to a semblance of caring undermined her defences. She floundered in a sea of confusing emotions.

He pressed his point. 'Last night you seemed keen to work with me.'

'I . . . I want to. It's just . . .'

'Tony didn't have any definite plans. He'll enjoy discussing art with my mother.'

She sighed and dropped her lashes, veiling her inner anguish. 'I don't like being pushed around as if my feelings don't count. I am a person, you know.'

'I know. And what you feel counts, Jenny. Far more than you realise.'

The soft sincerity in his voice brought a rush of blood to her cheeks. 'Well, it doesn't seem that way,' she mumbled self-consciously.

'Probably because you don't realise what a fascinating person you are. We all want your company and I didn't intend to lose my advantage this morning. However, that was probably selfish of me and if you want to go back to Tony . . .'

The rush of blood to her cheeks had continued to a wild circuit of her brain at the dizzying delight of those words. Her . . . a fascinating person? She looked at him in startled wonder. Did he really mean it? He had certainly insisted on her company.

'No. You're right. Tony'll be happy with his mother. Let's . . . let's get on with it,' she answered hurriedly.

He smiled and Jenny's heart curled with pleasure. He took her arm and led her into his bedroom, and immediately the pleasure cramped into pain. She stiffened away from him. Robert pretended not to notice her tension. He talked about music while he produced score-sheets and pencils and threaded the tape of her songs on to the player. She settled herself at the table he had placed for her convenience, then realised she did not have her guitar.

'Where are you going?'

The question cracked out, halting her movement. She looked back at him in surprise. The tautness of his body and the blazing intensity of his eyes held her tongue-tied for a moment.

'To ... to get my guitar,' she finally stammered.

He breathed a sigh of relief and his expression softened into apology. 'Don't be nervous of me, Jenny. I feel enough of a heel as it is.'

She flushed crimson. 'I can't help it.'

'Go and get your guitar. I promise you we'll work. Nothing else.'

And they did work. The tape was played and replayed as they went through each song. He pointed out phrases which displeased his ear and suggested variations that could improve the effect she had touched upon but not perfected. Jenny quickly picked up his suggestions, experimenting on her guitar and noting possible changes on score-sheets. Gradually music dominated her mind and a feeling of exhilaration crept into her heart as first one song and then another developed a more telling sound.

'You must have studied music yourself to have such a good ear, Robert,' she commented after he had raised a very technical point.

He gave her a sly grin. 'I used to play a mean clarinet in my student days, but I'm long out of practise.'

'Did you play in a band?'

'For a while,' he nodded. 'It was fun but didn't fully satisfy me. I wanted to do more and the wide scope of television attracted me. Dad had the contacts to help me get a start and I finally made it to where I wanted to be. I enjoy my work just as much as you enjoy your music. I like making a whole show come together into one artistic whole, and it irritates me enormously if it doesn't,' he added wryly.

She smiled. 'That seems to be a family characteristic.'

He raised his eyebrows questioningly.

'The drive for perfection in your work,' she explained.

'Yes, I guess we are pretty obsessive when it comes to achieving what we want.'

His eyes seemed to hold a possessive gleam as they held hers. Jenny's heart gave a great leap and she quickly looked away, anxious to hide her emotional reaction to the warmth he was projecting. Everything about Robert confused her. She did not understand him, could not relate his attitude of today to his actions of yesterday at all.

They worked on. There was no lack of understanding where music was concerned. They spoke the same language, held the same quick appreciation, immediately grasping what the other intended. Their communication was not only easy. It was an absolute joy to Jenny. She had never experienced anything like it before. Except yesterday. But then the sense of intimacy had been created without words, a fantasy which had led her badly astray. This was real.

It was Robert who called a halt. He was over by the window, looking down at the courtyard below. The back of the house formed a U, Annabel Knight's studio protruding on one side, the billiard room with Robert's bedroom above it on the other. This created a sheltered area which was a perfect suntrap for the swimming-pool.

'Everyone's sprawled out around the pool and Mrs Cherry has just wheeled out a buffet lunch. Are you hungry?'

'What time is it?' Jenny asked, amazed that it could be lunchtime already.

Robert glanced at his watch. 'One o'clock. We've been at it for almost four hours.'

Four hours. Was he now bored with her company? 'I didn't realise I'd taken up your whole morning,' she said in confused apology.

He smiled. 'Jenny, you could take up my whole day and I'd enjoy every minute of it. But I did agree to take you down to lunch and you need a break from concentration.'

He was right. She was mentally tired but she would never have admitted it if he had been willing to continue. 'Thank you for . . .'

'Don't thank me,' he insisted with a bemused shake of his head. 'I should be thanking you. You have a very generous nature, Jenny Ross, and I'm afraid that if we stay here much longer, I'll be in danger of imposing on it.'

He moved towards her as he spoke and Jenny could not quite believe the message in his eyes. Not after yesterday's rejection. She knew to her cost that an inexperienced virgin held no attraction for him, yet his expression seemed to deny this. She wondered wildly if it was her music which stirred him into thinking she was desirable. He stopped short of her as if sensing her reserve.

'Why don't we change into costumes and have a swim before lunch? Work up an appetite,' he suggested in a friendly fashion.

'Yes. I'd like that,' she answered jerkily. 'I'll see you down at the pool then.'

Her exit was swift, a purely defensive reaction to the disturbing force of Robert Knight. Back in her room she decided there was no point in trying to figure Robert out. His motivations were too obscure for a person of her limited experience. She pulled on her red bikini and then felt ridiculously self-conscious in it. Since Robert had seen her completely naked it seemed crazy to start being over-modest, but she slipped on a short towelling coat and immediately felt more comfortable.

The feeling did not last long. She opened her bedroom door and there was Robert waiting for her, leaning casually against the balustrade and wearing what could only be called a token pair of briefs. Jenny's pulse leapt into overtime as her eyes skittered over the body which had shared her nakedness yesterday. She could not meet his eyes.

'Ready?' he asked matter-of-factly.

She nodded, unable to trust her voice either.

He took her hand, quite naturally, as if her hand belonged to him. Jenny walked down the stairs, conscious of nothing but the feel of strong fingers enclosing hers. The warmth suffusing her body resulted in a deep, telling blush. The thought of facing the Knight family like this brought an agony of self-consciousness. She wriggled her fingers free and drifted apart from Robert as they reached the paved courtyard.

'About time too,' Tony grumbled, but his welcoming grin held no chagrin. 'I was about to go up and haul you out. Come and join me, Jenny, and bring some tucker with you.'

'Help yourself to whatever you want, Jenny,' Annabel Knight invited, waving to a buffet table where plates of salads and cold meats had been covered with protective cloths.

'We're going to have a swim first,' Robert said for both of them.

'Water's lovely,' Miranda called out.

Robert needed no further urging. He dived into the pool and began churning down its length in a professional crawl. Jenny hung back for a moment but Miranda's minute bikini gave her the confidence to discard her coat. She slid into the water by way of the steps and swam the length of the pool several times in a slow side-stroke, keeping well clear of Robert's wave-making. She had enough trouble coping with the emotional waves he churned up. She had already made a fool of herself with Robert Knight. It would be doubly foolish to lose her head again without looking carefully at where it would lead.

She did not wait for him to finish swimming. Her empty stomach demanded food. She loaded up a plate with coleslaw, baby potatoes, asparagus, pineapple, lettuce, tomato, and several slices of ham, then went to join Tony. There were several small casual tables on which to set her plate. Tony dragged one over to the sun-lounger next to his and she settled down to eat.

'Just look at that!' Miranda exclaimed, eyeing Jenny's plate with envy. 'And here I am, condemned to carrot and celery stalks! I bet you can eat anything you like all the time and never put on weight.'

'Pretty well,' Jenny agreed with a grin at Miranda's ample curves. 'But given the choice, I bet you wouldn't swap figures with me.'

'Now listen here!' Tony waved an admonishing finger at her. 'That's the last time I want to hear you putting yourself down or I'll toss you in the pool. Some men might fancy Miranda's ample flesh . . .'

'Well, thank you very much, brother mine,' Miranda flashed at him haughtily.

'. . . but a smaller scale is likewise appealing. Don't you agree with me, Rob?' he demanded as his brother heaved himself out of the water.

'Agree with what?' Robert asked, raking his wet hair back with his fingers.

'That Jenny has as much sex appeal as our femme fatale sister.'

'Delectable in every way,' he tossed off lightly, 'but right now, food has the most appeal. I'm starving.'

Jenny concentrated hard on her lunch. Her stomach had suddenly churned at Robert's choice of word. It recalled yesterday too sharply. He had murmured then that he wanted to taste all of her. Fortunately he did not linger to talk but moved straight to the buffet. When he eventually dropped into the lounger next to hers, Jenny had had time to fix her composure.

'This is the life!' he declared contentedly. 'Music in the morning, sun in the afternoon.'

'And what do you have lined up for tonight?' Tony drawled provocatively.

'More rest and relaxation.'

'You must be getting old, Rob.'

'I always preferred quality to quantity, Tony.'

'Really, you boys!' their mother sighed. 'Kindly raise the level of your conversation.'

'He's saving up his energy for New Year's Eve, Tony,' Miranda put in slyly. 'The studio boss is hosting a big party and everyone who's anyone in television is bound to be there. Rob'll be fending them off.'

'That should be something to see,' Tony grinned.

'Why don't you and Jenny come with us?' Miranda suggested brightly. 'I've got a separate invitation. Rob and I were going to go together, easier for freedom of circulation, but we can easily say you're my escort and Jenny's with Rob.'

'Jenny, would you like to go and mingle with the heavenly bodies?' Tony mocked. 'No moon, but plenty of stars twinkling their little hearts out.'

'I ... I don't think ... It's not fair on Robert ...'

'What's not fair on me?' he demanded with an amused twitch of his lips.

'Oh, you wouldn't want anyone to think you were with me,' she finished impatiently. 'I'm not sophisticated ...'

'That does it!' Tony thundered.

Before Jenny grasped the reason for his wrath she was scooped out of her chair and thrown into the pool. She came up spluttering only to find Tony leaning over the side with his hand ready to push her under again.

'Say you'll come to the party, you idiot woman, or I'll drown you,' he threatened.

Jenny kicked herself out of arm's reach. 'I

don't have anything suitable to wear,' she insisted.

'I don't care. It's a woman I'm taking, not a stupid dress. I'll drown that damned inferiority complex of yours if it's the last thing I do,' he yelled, preparing to dive in.

'Hold it, Tony! A woman has her pride,' Miranda interceded. 'I'll take you shopping, Jenny. I know all the snazzy little boutiques in the city that don't charge you the earth for an outfit.'

'Go and drown her, Tony,' Robert urged. 'She deserves it for that crack about my supposed super-ego.'

Jenny shrieked as Tony plunged in and grabbed her legs. Her mouth filled with water as he pulled her under. When he let her surface she coughed out what seemed like half the pool.

'You beast, Tony Knight!' she gasped. 'You just wait! I'll pay you back!'

'You and who else?' he grinned, flexing his muscles in readiness.

'Geronimo!' Peter yelled and took a flying leap onto Tony's back. 'Get him, Jenny!'

She immediately scooped as much water as she could up into Tony's face as he wrestled his young brother off. Then she turned tail and scuttled out of the pool, shrieking with laughter. Peter hindered Tony's efforts to catch her and she cavorted around the pool, mocking him.

'Oh, thank you, Peter. You're a gentleman. The age of chivalry is not dead when a gallant youth rushes to rescue a maiden in distress. It's a pity your brother is such a brute.'

Tony's arm lashed out and almost caught her

ankle but she skipped away in time. Everyone was laughing uproariously and Jenny retired to her chair with exaggerated dignity, patting her hair with a towel. Tony playfully cuffed Peter's head as they emerged from the pool. Then he dropped into an ape-like stance and glowered at Jenny. 'King Kong's revenge,' he growled.

'Enough, Tony,' his father laughed. 'I can't stand any more. You're giving me indigestion.'

Tony straightened, put his hands on his hips and raised a threatening eyebrow. 'No more nonsense about this party?'

'If Miranda will guide me into something glamorous, I'll come,' she promised.

Tony shook his head in mock despair. 'You don't need glamour, Jenny-wren. That's for women who have nothing else.' He dropped back into his lounger and sighed. 'Why won't women listen? Here I am, a foremost authority on what pleases a man, but they simply won't be told. Do you have this communication difficulty, Rob?'

'Not with Jenny.' He smiled at her and the warmth in his eyes was unmistakable. 'I can't remember when I've enjoyed a morning so much. How about we continue with the rest of your songs tomorrow, Jenny?'

'If you like,' she answered diffidently, inwardly exulting at the invitation but trying to repress her eagerness. Slowly, slowly, she cautioned herself.

'And let me add that I'd be pleased and proud to escort you anywhere and into any company. I respect you more than any woman I've met in a long time.'

'Wow! That's telling you, Jenny,' Miranda said on a note of incredulity. 'I never thought I'd hear such words coming from Rob. He's always been a hard-boiled cynic as far as the fair sex is concerned.'

'You'd better keep it at respect, big brother, if you understand me.'

The cold, clipped words dropped like icicles, freezing the conversation. Jenny shrank back in her lounger as she felt tension whip across her.

'Well, well, well,' Miranda breathed, looking from Tony to Rob and back again. 'What do we have here?'

'Shut up, Miranda!' Tony snapped.

'I'm not sure I do understand you,' Robert said slowly. 'Precisely what are you saying, Tony? I think you'd better spell it out.'

'You might be the music-man, Rob, but this song is mine. The tunes you play aren't in the right key for Jenny, so make damned sure you play them elsewhere. I wouldn't like us to fall out of harmony.'

Jenny writhed, not only with embarrassment, but with an instinctive protest against Tony's interference, however well-meant it was. Before she could voice her feelings, Edward Knight had smoothly intervened.

'Tony, Robert is not entirely lacking in perception—I hope. And talking of perception, I was reading a book on E.S.P. this morning. Extraordinary what they're doing with it these days. Do you know . . .' He rambled on, aided by a spate of interested questions from Peter.

Jenny lay back and closed her eyes. Every nerve-end seemed to be jangling and for a while she simply concentrated on relaxing. There was no point in stewing over a situation that was out of her control. Tony had no right to warn his brother off, but having been made painfully aware of Robert's casual attitude to sex, she understood Tony's motives. She was here at his invitation and he obviously felt responsible for her well-being.

The warning was too late but he was not to know that. Robert was a man who took what he wanted. The only snag was that he had not wanted a virgin. So now he respected her. The irony of it all was almost funny, but Jenny could not find any laughter.

Tony suddenly loomed over her with a large sun-umbrella and proceeded to set it into a special slot in the paving behind her. 'Better watch that fair skin. Don't want you suffering from sunburn.'

Apparently she had awakened all his protective instincts this afternoon. She thanked him with an affectionate smile. Tony had always been good to her, thoughtful and kind. He threw her a happy grin and again she wondered why it was Robert and not Tony who stirred her heart. In comparison to his brother, Tony had a far less complicated personality and he had so many attractive qualities. She sighed and closed her eyes again.

Everyone lazed through the afternoon, occasionally having a swim but mostly content to lie in the sun, drink cold drinks and engage in desultory conversation Robert was the most silent and the most inactive. When he was not apparently sleeping, he listened without joining in and observed whatever was happening from under lazy lids, making it impossible to know what he was thinking. Several times Jenny felt an intense gaze on her, but when she turned to him his expression seemed to hold disinterest. She hid her frustration by responding warmly to Tony's good-humoured banter.

During dinner that night Robert's withdrawn air was even more pronounced. Jenny heard Annabel Knight remarking on it questioningly but Robert's reply was too soft for Jenny to hear. He did not accompany them to the lounge and the rest of the evening seemed flat and meaningless to Jenny. She wryly concluded that even if Robert's presence discomforted her, she would prefer to suffer it than not have it at all.

He was at breakfast when she went downstairs the next morning. After a polite greeting he asked if she would like to continue working on her songs. Her heart leapt with eagerness and her answer was firmly positive. By nine o'clock they were settled in his bedroom again.

Their work-session was exactly that, total concentration on improving her songs. Not once did Robert relax into a more personal vein. His quiet intensity of purpose pressured Jenny to try harder all the time. Finally there was only the 'Wishing' song which remained unsatisfactory. Robert had been persisting with it for almost an hour when Jenny put down her guitar and shook her head.

'It's no use. I can't think any more. I'll have to get away from it for a while.'

He nodded and switched off the equipment they had been using. 'Would you like a drink?'

'Yes, please.' She felt wrung out from all the concentrated effort and nursed a little hope that

Robert might now be more responsive to her as a person.

He poured out a gin and tonic and handed it to her. Jenny felt self-conscious accepting it but Robert did not even glance at her. He opened a can of beer for himself and wandered over to the window, seemingly restless.

'I don't think I can give you any more help on that one, Jenny, and I'll be back at the studio from tomorrow until New Year,' he stated matter-of-factly.

A little frisson of unease swept through Jenny. There was something in his tone and manner which suggested finality, as if he was announcing the end of their association. And she desperately wanted it to continue.

He swung around to face her. His expression had a shuttered look as if his thoughts were turned in upon himself. 'That's why I wanted to get through as much as we could this morning. You'll keep trying with the "Wishing" song?' he pressed, his eyes darting anxiously at her.

It was a struggle to rise above the rolling wave of desolation. 'Yes. Yes, I suppose so,' she forced out, then drew in a quick breath to settle her nausea. 'It will probably nag at me until I get it right.'

'It's going to be the best, but the others are ready to sell now, Jenny.'

That jolted her. 'Sell?'

He frowned at her reaction. 'Don't you realise they can earn you a lot of money?'

She felt even sicker. Robert Knight had spent these last two mornings with her out of

professional interest. She dragged through her
memory for the words he had used. He had said
he wanted to share her music. That was all. That
had been his only purpose. Nothing personal at
all. She was a fool, letting a fantasy of hope
colour the starkness of reality. 'Who would buy
them?' she muttered dispiritedly.

'I can think of several people who would be
interested.'

She shook her head. 'I wouldn't know how to
go about it.'

'I have the contacts. If you like, I could act as
your agent.'

She was not sure she could stand any more
professional contact with Robert. Her feelings
towards him were not the least bit businesslike.
'No, I don't think so,' she sighed.

'Why not?'

'I don't feel like putting my music on the
chopping-block to be dissected by outsiders,' she
said with a touch of resentment at his impersonal
manner.

'Jenny, it won't be dissected,' he said earnestly.
'Believe me! Your music is good. Better than
good. I'm sure that every song will be snapped
up. All you'll have to do . . .'

'I'll think about it,' she cut in irritably. Then
she pulled herself together and put a polite mask
on her face to cover her retreat with dignity.
'Thank you for your interest, Robert. It was good
of you to give me so much of your time.'

She carefully laid the untouched drink aside,
gathered her work-sheets together, then bent to
pick up her guitar. When she rose to her feet it
was to find that Robert had moved closer to her.

His forehead was creased in concern. He gestured an appeal.

'Jenny, I assure you that your songs are readily acceptable.'

'Thank you. You're very kind,' she replied stiltedly.

'I'm not being kind,' he grated out in frustration. 'I'm telling you the truth.'

'I said I'd think about it.'

For one tense moment he looked as if he wanted to shake her. Then he expelled his breath in a hissing sigh. 'All right. Let me know if you come to a decision. I'll help you in any way I can.' His mouth curved into a wry smile. 'As for working with you, it was a pleasure, Jenny. It's not often that one feels completely in tune with a person.'

The remark stabbed straight to her heart. 'You felt that?' The question accused him of rejecting something which should have been welcomed, valued, nurtured.

He made a dismissive gesture as if annoyed with himself. 'Why not? We both have a deep appreciation of music. It's pleasant to share the same understanding.'

Intuition argued that he was deliberately downplaying an attraction which even now was playing havoc with her emotions. But intuition had played her false before and she did not have enough confidence to challenge him. His first rejection had been too cutting to risk another.

'Yes, very pleasant,' she echoed dully. 'Thanks again, Robert.' With a little nod of acknowledgment she turned and walked out of the room, her head held high, her hopes shrivelled into dust.

She saw very little of Robert over the next few days. He spent long hours at the television studio, preparing a musical extravaganza which was to be pre-recorded for New Year's Eve. He said 'good morning' at breakfast and was occasionally home in time to bid her goodnight. That was the sum of their intercourse.

Jenny found it difficult to understand why he had encouraged her so warmly when now he barely acknowledged her existence. Hurt and frustration were gnawing pains which could not be dismissed. Had the warmth merely been the flirtatious charm which Robert adopted for women in general? After many hours of agonising over the change in his manner, Jenny finally pinpointed when Robert had started withdrawing that warmth. It was after Tony's warning, 'play your tunes elsewhere'. It would seem now that Robert had only been amusing himself with her, playing on her heartstrings, enjoying her obvious vulnerability to him. If so, Tony had been right to interfere. Except that she craved for the tune to be played again.

The fact that Tony danced close attendance on her was no consolation for Robert's defection, but it did provide distraction and for that Jenny was grateful. He set out a programme which ensured that Jenny was shown every treat the city had to offer from Paddy's Markets to lunch in the Centrepoint Tower. One day Miranda overrode Tony's plans and took Jenny shopping. Jenny was dazzled by the stunning range of clothes in one boutique after another and was finally persuaded into buying a daring little outfit for the New Year's Eve party. When they arrived home

Tony declared that since he had been left alone all day, Jenny had to spend a night on the town with him.

He nagged her into accepting with a blend of down-in-the-mouth accusation and charming persuasion, then took her to one of the most expensive nightclubs at King's Cross. Jenny's protests at the outrageous cost of everything were laughingly disregarded. He plied her with champagne and kept her laughing with non-stop nonsense. She even forgot Robert for a while.

Jenny had never been to such a glamorous place and it was quite an exciting experience. The entertainment comprised a world-class singer and a popular comedian, the band of musicians was very good, the food an adventure in itself, and Tony made sure that her glass was always full. They danced until the small hours and she was too fuzzy-headed to object when he tucked her against him during the taxi-ride home. He felt warm and comfortable. Even when he brushed his mouth against her hair she only sighed and snuggled closer.

'Have a good time, Jenny-wren?' he murmured.

'Mmm. Thanks Tony.'

When they arrived home she readily accepted his support up the stairs. At her door he turned her into a gentle embrace and dropped a kiss on her forehead. It was nice. Tony was nice. It did not occur to her to protest when he tilted her chin and brushed her lips with his.

'G'night, Tony,' she whispered drowsily. 'Thanks again.'

He muttered words she did not catch. For a

moment his arms tightened but he let her go before she thought to question the pressure.

She refused his invitations for further nights out, despite his arguments and obvious disappointment. Jenny did not want to be in his debt, nor did she want Tony to begin treating her as a date. Their relationship meant a great deal to her as it was and she did not want its parameters becoming blurred. Tony was not one to sulk. He continued to sweep her into a variety of daytime activities which left her little time on her own.

The few hours which she had alone Jenny spent working on the 'Wishing' song. A sense of pride insisted on getting it right. Somehow it was tied up with proving her music worthy of Robert's accolades. And still there was the niggling need to win back his interest, even if it was only professional interest.

It was the day before New Year's Eve when a burst of inspiration produced exactly the sound she had been searching for. It was right. It was perfect. She wanted to rush out and tell someone but only Robert would appreciate precisely what she had achieved. Above all, she wanted to share it with him. All day she waited in a fever of impatience. Disappointment ruined her appetite when he did not come home for dinner. The evening dragged. One by one the family retired for the night. Jenny had to follow suit. She tried to read, far too restless to sleep.

It was almost midnight when she heard Robert come in. She put down her book and ran to her door, wanting to fling it open and rush out to him. A dozen inhibitions squashed the impulse. She stood behind her door in an agony of uncertainty. His footsteps sounded weary as he mounted the stairs. He had to be very tired after such a long day. His mind would still be turned on to his work. Maybe he would brush her off. Maybe he would just smile and nod and ... she wanted so much more from him.

He was walking along the corridor. His footsteps sounded just outside her room. She had to act now if she was going to tell him. Now ... now ... Every nerve quivered. Her hand was clammy as it grasped the knob. Her fingers slipped, weak, useless. It was too late. She closed her eyes and listened to Robert's door clicking shut. She sighed. It had been stupid to get all worked up. His door was shut to her anyway. One song would not prise it open.

All the elation she had felt faded away and a vast hollowness grew in its place. She undressed, switched off the light and went to bed. There was no point in yearning for what Robert Knight could give her. He was not prepared to give it. She had held out all her gifts. They had not been enough to keep his interest. And yet ... somehow she found it so difficult to accept that he was indifferent to her. He had seemed so intent on sharing a relationship with her when he spoke on Christmas night. Had it only been professional interest?

Jenny tossed and turned, as restless as her thoughts. Her mind finally fastened on the party for New Year's Eve. Robert would surely be spending some time in her company. His manner to her tomorrow night might resolve some of her questions. And maybe ... if she could show him ... With a persistent little hope worming into her heart, Jenny began making plans.

CHAPTER SEVEN

'HAVEN'T you finished titivating yet?' Tony called through the door.

'We won't be long. Go on down. We'll meet you in the lounge,' Jenny said firmly.

'Just what are you girls up to in there?'

'You'll see. We'll be worth waiting for,' Miranda declared smugly.

The two girls grinned at each other in the mirror as Tony went off, grumbling loudly about women's foibles. Miranda was skilfully winding long tresses of Jenny's hair around her curling wand, intent on achieving the effect she had planned. Jenny had bought a little, gold-mesh cap for covering a chignon. Miranda had stuffed this with a false hair-piece, cut a hole in the top and drawn Jenny's pony-tail through it. The pony-tail was now getting special treatment.

Jenny could hardly believe the exotic look Miranda had given her face. It was no longer ordinary. Green eyeshadow and brown eyeliner tilted the corners of her eyes and an artistic finish of gold eyeshadow gave them even more emphasis. A special foundation masked most of her freckles and a subtle peach colouring on her cheeks highlighted cheekbones which Jenny had always ignored. Even her mouth looked luscious, outlined with a dark coral and filled in with peach gloss.

Miranda had lent her a necklace and earrings of

delicate gold leaves which gave just the right Oriental touch to her outfit. The harem pants looked soft and very feminine in a glowing, gold material, and the tight-fitting bolero pushed her breasts up into a slight swell above the low, rounded neckline. A sash of gold satin accentuated her tiny waist.

Jenny stared at her reflection with a mixture of elation and apprehension. Robert could not say that this girl did not fit into his sophisticated world and Jenny was determined to act the part Miranda had dressed her for. Her fear was that Robert might not appreciate the change.

It had been very late last night by the time she had figured out her mistakes. She had to be positive to keep Robert's interest alive, not a shrinking violet. She had to show him she could fit into the society he was used to. And she would sell her songs. She would accept Robert's offer to be her agent. Then he would have to spend time with her, time which would increase her chances of understanding his needs.

'That's it!' Miranda declared, curving one last tress on to Jenny's shoulder.

'Thank you, Miranda. I can't tell you how much I appreciate all your help. You've made me look ... I've just never looked as good as this in my life. It's ... it's almost like a miracle.'

Miranda laughed. 'Tricks of the trade, Jenny. I must say I did do a good job. You look absolutely stunning.'

Miranda, herself, looked superb in a gauze blue-and-silver caftan which floated over a skintight silver bodysuit. Without a doubt she was a show-stopper with her perfect curves, but

Jenny was no longer envious. Miranda had indeed made her look stunning and a new surge of confidence brought an added sparkle to her sparkling eyes. She could not stop smiling at her reflection in the mirror as she dabbed on some perfume. She caught Miranda's grin and laughed.

'I can't help it. I can't believe it's me.'

Miranda picked up their evening-bags and handed Jenny hers. 'Come on. We'll make a grand entrance into the lounge and knock their eyes out.'

Robert had been at the studio all day. Jenny had not seen him since breakfast this morning when they had exchanged a polite greeting. He had barely looked at her. But she was confident that he would look at her now. Her eyes sought him as soon as she and Miranda stepped into the lounge. He was standing with his father near the drinks cabinet.

'Well, here we are!' Miranda announced. 'You'd better all drool accordingly and say we were worth waiting for.'

Edward Knight immediately turned a smile upon them. Robert was slower to react. Eager for his approval, Jenny willed him to smile too. The impassive face held little expression until his eyes skated over Jenny. Then surprise raised his eyebrows. They quickly lowered into a slight frown. Jenny's heart lurched. Had dressing up been another mistake, she worried frantically. In the same instant, Tony's appalled voice shattered the confidence she had so painstakingly constructed.

'My God! You bloody fool, Miranda! You might as well have given her seven veils too.

Then she could've hidden that mask of a face you've plastered on her.'

'Tony!' Annabel Knight's shocked reprimand made no impression on him.

'Tarted up like any cheap whore! Salome, for God's sake!'

'Tony!' his father bellowed.

'Well, where the hell is she? Answer me that!' he retorted fiercely. 'She's not even there any more. It's someone else. One of the plastic people!'

Shock had held her rigid under Tony's savage onslaught of words. Then her eyes turned to Robert in a desperate plea for him to deny his brother's judgment. His gaze was fixed on Tony, his lips thinned in anger. There were voices raised in outrage against Tony's rude outburst; Miranda's, Annabel and Edward Knight's, but not Robert's. Not Robert's. He said nothing. No rush to her defence. No reproof to his brother. No sympathetic look at her. Just thin-lipped disapproval of the whole scene.

Jenny's shining bubble of hope burst. Tears sprang into her eyes. She backed away, her heart thumping a wild protest at the pain coursing through it. Then she turned and ran, almost falling up the stairs in her haste to get away. She had failed. Failed. Failed. The word was a tattoo of despair in her brain, carving itself relentlessly deeper with every step she stumbled over.

'Jenny!'

Tony's shout rang in her ears and pounded into her head. She ran into the bathroom and locked the door. Dazedly, as if in some horrible nightmare, she staggered over to the vanity and stared at the mirror. Tears were carving through her pancake make-up in dirty, mascaraed streams. She grabbed a handful of tissues and started rubbing, smearing the eyeshadow. The face of a weird clown looked back at her. Someone hammered at the door and shouted words. Jenny blocked the noise out of her mind. She needed soap and water. The tissues weren't enough. She fumbled with the taps. Her hands were shaking uncontrollably.

It seemed to take a long time to clean her face of every last trace of make-up. There were more voices outside the door. Jenny ignored them. She scrubbed at her skin until the freckles showed out starkly across her cheeks and nose. Then she unpinned the false chignon and the gold-mesh cap and dragged her hair free of them. Her fingers raked out the sculptured pony-tail, pulling the long tresses forward. She carefully removed Miranda's necklace and earrings, then stripped off her clothes, seeing them now as a fancy dress costume.

Having wrapped herself in a huge bath-towel, Jenny lifted her chin proudly and opened the door. Tony and his mother stood just outside, concern on Annabel Knight's face and wretched apology on her son's.

'Please excuse me,' Jenny said with brittle dignity. 'You can tell the others I won't be long, Tony. I only have to put a dress on and brush my hair.'

Tony's hand came down on her shoulder as she attempted to brush past. 'Jenny,' he murmured, his tone deeply anxious.

'Please don't delay me,' she said stiffly, holding

herself rigid and keeping her eyes fixed on her bedroom door.

'Let go, Tony,' his mother said with quiet authority.

His hand slid away and Jenny walked quickly to her room, her head held high. Without hesitation she drew a simple, yellow shift from the wardrobe and zipped it on. The soft crepe loosely hugged her body and the dress had a plain elegance which made it passable for most occasions. It was not stunning or even eye-catching, but it was passable. She was vigorously attacking her hair when Annabel Knight knocked and walked in, the harem pants and bolero hanging over her arm.

'Jenny dear, I'm so sorry,' she said feelingly, clearly distressed by the situation.

Jenny swallowed hard and forced herself to speak politely. 'I'm sorry for making a scene, Mrs Knight.'

'The scene was not of your making. I can only hope you'll be able to forgive Tony his incredibly bad manners. He is extremely sorry for being so hurtful.'

'Truthful,' Jenny corrected bitterly. Tears filmed her eyes again. 'He was just being truthful, Mrs Knight, and I don't hold it against him. Better to have made a fool of myself here than at a whole party of people.'

'You weren't making a fool of yourself, Jenny. You looked very charming. Quite exotic, actually. It was just that you looked so different and he wasn't expecting it.'

Jenny shook her head as she carefully plucked at the long hairs caught in the brush needles.

'No. He was right. I was trying to make myself into something I'm not. He shouldn't have blamed Miranda. I asked her to do it. I wanted to show . . .' She drew in a shuddering breath and let it out in a despondent sigh. 'I was wrong. Hopelessly wrong. It wasn't only Tony. It was on Robert's face too.' She attacked her hair again, her eyes glittering with wounded pride.

'Then I can't persuade you to change back into these clothes. You did look lovely in them, Jenny,' she added kindly.

'I couldn't wear them now, Mrs Knight. I'll have to do as I am.' She put down the brush and turned around, her lips curved in a brave attempt at a smile. 'Tony did say he was taking the woman and not the dress. Fine feathers aren't really my style. He calls me a wren. And that's what I am, a small, brown, speckled bird. I can't even pretend to be a peacock.'

Annabel Knight dropped the clothes on the bed and walked over to Jenny. She took her hands and squeezed them gently. Her face was soft with compassion. 'Peacocks are cold, proud birds with ugly, grating voices. Wrens are far more lovable, Jenny, and we've loved having you here with us.' She leaned forward and kissed Jenny's cheek in a motherly fashion. 'Now, may I send Tony up to make his peace with you? He is stewing in absolute misery.'

'I have to face them all, Mrs Knight. I'd rather do it in one go. I'll be down in a minute. I think I left my evening-bag in the bathroom.'

'No, it's there on the bed. I brought it in with your clothes.'

'Then I'll come down with you.'

Jenny picked up her bag and accompanied Annabel Knight down the stairs. Tony was hovering near the doorway into the lounge. He started towards them, looking at Jenny with an agony of uncertainty on his face.

She forced a smile. 'Do I look better now?'

'I am most dreadfully sorry, Jenny,' he said with deep feeling. 'You should have slapped me across the face or kicked my shins, done all the things you've ever threatened me with. I can only say . . .' He lifted his hands in apologetic appeal. 'All that make-up. It was like a sacrilege . . . I love your face just as it is . . . and to replace it with gunks of paint . . .'

'Tony, I don't think you're doing very well,' his mother interrupted sternly.

'I'm trying to explain,' he said desperately. 'I didn't think. I felt so angry . . . so . . .'

Jenny placed a soothing hand on his arm. 'It's all right, Tony. I understand. Truly I do.'

He searched her face intently then pulled her into his arms, rocking her in a tender embrace. 'Oh, Jenny love, I wouldn't hurt you for the world. And here I've blundered all over your female pride like a prize idiot. I'm sorry, sweetheart.'

She rested her head against his chest and sighed, accepting the warm comfort of his body. The deathly chill around her heart could not be reached, but that was not Tony's fault. He had simply made her face reality.

'Do you truly want to go to this party?' he asked gently. 'If you'd rather . . .'

'Yes. I want to go.' She wanted to see Robert's world even if she did not belong in it.

Tony drew back and tilted her chin up. His eyes shone with affection and admiration. 'In that case, let me tell you I'll have the most beautiful woman there at my side.'

'Who? Miranda?' she deliberately teased.

He bared his teeth and then relaxed into a grin. 'No. I've done enough shaking up for one night. But one day, Jenny Ross, I'll make you believe me.'

She smiled and the smile did not need to be forced this time. 'I believe you believe it, Tony. Come on,' she urged, slipping her arm around his. 'I've kept everyone waiting long enough as it is.'

Chagrin was uppermost in Miranda's expression as she took in the changes of Jenny's appearance. Resentment burnt in her eyes as she glared at Tony. 'Well, I hope you're satisfied, big-mouth brother,' she said scornfully.

'Miranda, I know you must think that all your time and efforts have been wasted,' Jenny said tactfully, 'but I enjoyed what you did for me at the time, and I'm grateful to you for the experience. But the truth is, I am more comfortable as myself, so please don't be mad at us.'

'I'm not mad at you, Jenny. Only at my big oaf of a brother who suffers from an acute case of foot-in-mouth disease, not to mention . . .'

'All right, all right,' Tony protested. 'I've given Jenny *carte blanche* to hang and quarter me, but she insists on going to the party. So, Rob, are you driving us or are we going in separate cars?'

'Take the Mercedes if you like,' Edward Knight offered. 'It'd be more comfortable than trying to squeeze into Robert's Porsche. And, Jenny, may I say you look like a breath of spring in a deadly hot summer.'

'Thank you, Mr Knight,' she smiled, still carefully avoiding Robert's eye. She had managed the situation quite smoothly so far and once they were in the darkness of a travelling car she could relax the tight hold she had on her emotions. To risk looking at Robert now would be unnecessarily foolhardy. If he showed amusement or pity she would be sick.

Robert drove the Mercedes. Miranda took the passenger seat in the front and Jenny sat next to Tony in the back. For the first few minutes they travelled in silence. Jenny stared at the back of Robert's head, silently agonising over the débâcle of her attempt at sophistication. She was unaware that she was picking at her fingernails. Tony suddenly reached a hand across and stopped her.

She sighed and gave him a wry look. 'Sorry. Old habit.'

He grinned. 'Can't stand the sound of it. I was just thinking. How about we go back home tomorrow?'

'To Nangoa? I thought you wanted to stay with your parents until after New Year.'

'Well, tomorrow's New Year anyway.'

Jenny's heart shrank into a smaller lump of ice. Even if it had been possible to recover from tonight's foolishness, there would be no more time with Robert. 'Whatever you like,' she said flatly.

'There you go again, Tony,' Miranda flung over her shoulder. 'Only thinking of yourself.

Mum's been looking forward to having you with her for at least two weeks, and here you are talking about cutting your visit short.'

'I doubt that she'll mind, Miranda,' Robert said in a soft, toneless voice. 'She has seen him.'

'I can't see why Tony has to rush off tomorrow anyhow,' Miranda retorted petulantly.

Robert wanted her to go. Jenny sensed the wish behind the words. It was finished. There was no hope any more.

'Mum will understand, Miranda,' Tony said with easy confidence. 'I've got the itch to get back to work so I'd only be restless if I stay. You don't mind, do you, Jenny?'

'No. I don't mind,' she answered quietly.

'Then what say we sleep in tomorrow morning, have lunch with the family, then get an early afternoon start?'

'All right.'

It was settled. With dull resignation she totalled up the hours left. Eighteen at most, and half that would be spent in sleep. She could probably only count on Robert's company for the party tonight and lunch tomorrow. Even that she would have to share. No time alone with him. Not that it mattered. He didn't want her anyway. She swallowed a sigh and began composing herself for the evening ahead of her.

As it turned out she did not have Robert's company for the party either. As soon as they were welcomed into their host's home Tony took charge of her.

'Don't worry about us, Rob. You and Miranda go and do your thing. If we want an introduction to someone we'll come and ask, but Jenny and I are just going to enjoy ourselves, observing the *hoi polloi* at play.'

'Hey! There's Trevor Jacquard,' Miranda said excitedly, smiling and waving to a very handsome man who was on the other side of the room. He wriggled his fingers back at her. 'See you later. I'm off,' she declared happily and weaved her way through the crowd.

'This is not entirely a social evening for me, so if you're sure that's what you want, Tony, I'll get about my business,' Robert said off-handedly. He gave Jenny a formal nod. His face looked stiff and wooden, void of any telling expression. 'I'll catch up with you both later.'

Then he was gone too. Jenny saw him hailed by a group of people and he was quickly swallowed up in their midst. Well, she had wanted answers, she told herself. Now she had them. Underlined. Nothing could have been more emphatic than Robert's determined role of non-participation in her life.

CHAPTER EIGHT

'LET'S take a walk around and have a look at the house,' Tony suggested cheerfully. 'It's supposed to be the product of creative genius. Brilliant architect at his best. Luxury house of the year sort of thing.'

Jenny pulled herself together. She had brought this situation upon herself through wishful thinking. Now she had to ride with it. She glanced around and made a remark on the most visible architectural feature. 'Well, that certainly is an impressive spiral staircase.' It was a massive, white, concrete structure with wide, shallow steps, brilliantly carpeted in red.

'Mmm,' Tony hummed consideringly. 'I would have to say it was solid. Like a great, white elephant. It kind of trumpets money, doesn't it? Very poor taste.'

Jenny threw him a wry look. Tony loved tearing down people who paraded their wealth on what he considered useless things. Objects of art were another matter altogether. Any amount of money could be spent on them with his benevolent approval.

The house itself made a good talking point. It was startlingly modern in concept with its wide expanses of glass cut in unusual shapes. The architect certainly had a geometrical bent. The main entertainment room was octagonal. All the furniture seemed angular and made of a mixture of leather, chrome and glass. Tony declared it smart and showy but lacking in homeliness. Jenny agreed with him. The house was an ultra-modern showpiece, interesting to look at but hardly relaxing to live in.

Jenny thought of her own small, shabby home and decided she was not envious. She would not be comfortable in this environment. The small-town atmosphere of Nangoa was more to her liking; ordinary people going about their hum-drum lives, getting married, having children, enjoying simple pleasures. There was nothing simple here.

She glanced around at the women's fashions and ironically noted that her harem pants and bolero would not have turned an eye. Glitter was all the mode and it seemed that anything was acceptable, from skintight leotards to dresses which hung perilously together on strings. Most of the men indulged in a dash of the theatrical, too, with ruffled shirts, gold chains, even satin trousers.

Tony pointed out various celebrities, making Jenny's lips twitch with his wickedly amusing comments. He was good company and in spite of her inner misery Jenny responded to his humour. Occasionally they spied Miranda and Robert among the crowd of milling guests. Miranda was always surrounded by men and Robert invariably had a couple of glamorous women clinging to him. No one took any notice of Tony and Jenny as they wandered around.

Tony spied a gallery of paintings on an upper level and suggested they take a peek. They idled around them whilst Tony gave voice to some scathing rhetoric. He considered modern abstracts pure commercialism, a prostitution of art. He was criticising a particularly vivid canvas when a cold, haughty voice interrupted.

'And what pretentious little credentials do you have for making such a glib judgment of my work?'

They swung around to be confronted by a woman whose appearance was so way out on the fringes of theatre, that Jenny's mouth dropped open in astonishment. She was almost as tall as Tony. Her make-up was wildly exaggerated and the Afro-frizz of red-gold hair was positively electric. Her head alone was stunning enough but the rest of her was equally startling. The slim body was draped in lounging pyjamas which were geometrically patterned in purple, pink and orange.

With supreme contempt, the woman looked Tony up and down. 'Undoubtedly mud on the brain. That's the usual drawback to gorgeous lumps of clay,' she added with biting derision.

Tony's face broke into a wide grin. 'Well, well, well! What do we have here?' he drawled mockingly. 'The hair reminds me of hissing snakes but since you haven't turned me into stone, it can't be Medusa.'

Jenny bit her lips to stifle the giggle which tickled her throat.

'Do you fancy yourself as Hercules with all those bulging muscles? Pity it's all brawn,' the woman retorted, not the least bit ruffled by Tony's jab at her appearance.

'I know you'll find it extraordinary, Madam, but I'm completely at ease with my body and my

face. I have no urge to disfigure or disguise it
with bizarre colourings.' He cocked his head on
one side consideringly. 'Though I do believe
you've missed out on a shade of puce. You've
done much better with your painting here. All
colours accounted for.' He swung back to the
maligned work and peered at the signature in
the corner. 'No. Not Medusa. Looks like ...
uh-oh!'

He straightened up and rolled his eyes at
Jenny. 'I think I've just put my foot in it again.
She's the daughter of the house.'

'And might I ask who you are, big-foot?'

Tony took Jenny's arm and posed with
exaggerated formality. 'Miss Flemming, may I
present my companion, Miss Jenny Ross.' He
bowed. 'Anthony Frederick Knight ... not quite
at your service.'

A gurgle of laughter greeted his introduction.
'Of course! The male-image of Miranda. And
brother to the super-sophisticated Robert Knight.
The tongue is just as quick but not so smooth.'

'I've always considered it a pity to blunt a
sharp instrument.'

She grinned at him, appreciating the dry wit.
'Let me tell you something, Anthony Frederick
Knight. I do as I please, and whatever anyone
else thinks about me doesn't matter a damn.
However, my pet hate is ill-informed art critics.'

'Strange! So's mine,' Tony agreed with
sardonic emphasis.

She folded her arms and looked askance at him.
One finely arched eyebrow rose higher. 'An
artist?'

'A better one than you'll ever be, if you're

content with that.'

'Indeed? I can't recall your name being publicised at any art gallery. You must be one of the great undiscovered. Don't you think it's sad the way people who can't make it to the top console themselves by tearing down the work of those who do?'

'The top!' Tony's voice had lost its lilt of humour.

Jenny squeezed his arm warningly but he paid no attention.

'My God! Your work, Miss Flemming, is a reflection of yourself. It captures the eye with its impact of primary colour. It is a decorator's piece, superficial frou-frou. I'm sure you sell well. Both you and your work would appeal to the plastic people. But quality, Miss Flemming, does not tire the eye. The more one looks at it the more entranced one becomes. Please excuse us. Looking at you has given me retina-fatigue.'

He marched Jenny away, making a bee-line for the glass doors which led out on to the patio. He snatched a drink from the tray of a passing waiter, paused to down it, then continued right on until they were beyond the main crowd of people.

'Aah! Fresh air!' he breathed.

'A bit hot under the collar, Tony?' Jenny teased.

'That witch of a woman!' he muttered. 'Smart, know-it-all bitch! Just wait till I'm ready for an exhibition!' His mouth curved into a grim smile. 'I'll send her a specially worded invitation. That's what I'll do. Very specially worded for Miss technicolour Flemming.'

Jenny grinned at him. 'I liked her. I thought she was rather marvellous.'

Tony shook his head at her. 'Jenny-wren, everything that glitters is not gold. And that was pure brass. Let's find some food. I'm hungry.'

An elaborate smorgasbord was set out for guests to help themselves whenever they wished. Waitresses stood by to serve hot dishes. Tony piled up his plate as if he had not eaten all day. Jenny did not feel like eating at all but she took a few delicacies just to show interest. They returned to the patio which ran the length of the house. There were tables and chairs at one end. At the other a dais had been set up for the band which was playing lively pop-music. It was pleasant to sit out-of-doors and Jenny did not feel compelled to put on a bright face in the dimmer light.

Having satisfied his hunger Tony turned his attention to the music. Whenever a particularly jazzy beat tempted him he drew Jenny into dancing. As midnight approached more and more guests drifted outside. The drum rolled in anticipation and one of the singers counted off the last seconds of the old year. Then cymbals clashed, bells rang, and a trumpet began the first notes of 'Should Auld Acquaintance Be Forgot'.

There was a confusion of loud merriment as people sang, whistled and shouted greetings. She exchanged a laughing kiss with Tony as they were showered with balloons and streamers. Her eyes darted hopefully around the crowd but there was no sign of Robert. Not even a New Year's kiss from him, she thought miserably.

Eventually the New Year's celebrations

subsided. The band retired for a well-earned break. The crowd outside thinned and Jenny spotted Robert in a group of people near the dais but he did not look her way. Tony muttered something to her and strode down the patio towards his brother. Anticipation squeezed her heart. Disappointment deflated the tension. Tony did not even look at Robert. He went straight to the dais, picked up a guitar and returned to her, bearing it in his arms like a gift.

'Play me a song, Jenny-wren. Here we are, out under the stars on a balmy summer's night. I have a fancy to hear the pleasant plunk of a guitar and your sweet voice.'

She was shaking her head.

'Please?'

'You'd better take it back before the owner returns.' She glanced towards the dais, anxious that the guitar not be missed. Her gaze automatically skated past Robert and halted. He was looking at her. As soon as their eyes locked he turned away. Hurt by what seemed a deliberate snub, Jenny's pride rose in revolt. 'On the other hand, I don't suppose one song would hurt.'

'That's the spirit,' Tony grinned. He handed over the guitar, threw a cushion on to the patio and sat down in front of her, face beaming with encouragement.

Without giving herself time to have second thoughts, Jenny played the rippling introduction on the guitar. Then with all the confidence of knowing that the melody had been perfected, her voice produced the purity of sound which was the 'Wishing' song. She gave all her stifled emotions free rein, and the haunting tune gathered a heart-catching momentum as it soared and drifted and soared again in its first long crescendo, reaching slowly upwards with all the yearning of a soul in torment, wishing for dreams which remained forever out of reach. The top note shivered on the air, a poignant cry of frustration, still echoing above the long, winding, cadence of despair.

As she played the chords which ushered in the second verse, Tony mumbled a few words. Jenny raised her lashes and looked at him. The gentle loving in his eyes was balm to her inner pain. A movement at the edge of her vision caught her attention and a darted glance showed that Robert had come forward. Knowing that she had captured his interest at last, Jenny poured more intensity into her voice, giving the lyrics and the music all the emotions which had ravaged her soul since loving him; the yearning, the unfulfilled promise, elation rising to a joyous trill, then twisting down a spiral of hopelessness, failure a flat monotone at the bottom of the scale.

She was unaware of people shuffling forward, unaware of the hushed silence which had grown around her, a watching, listening crowd which held its breath in awe. The song had her total concentration. It owned her. It was her. Her voice climbed the last arpeggio with a husky mournfulness, then slipped slowly down, the words barely a whisper, yet each dying phrase a sigh of longing which found recognition in every heart that had ever loved, the desolate cry of need which is rarely spoken.

The last upturned note of wistful hope hung

alone, echoing above the final thrum of the
guitar. There was an absolute stillness which
urged the echo to go on echoing. No one moved.
It seemed that no one breathed. All was waiting
silence.

Jenny did not know she was receiving the
ultimate accolade that any performer could be
given. She felt completely spent, emptied of
feeling. She raised weary eyes and looked straight
at Robert. The stunned expression on his face
was hollow satisfaction for all that she had poured
forth. It was no answer to her need. She closed
her eyes.

There was a soft sighing, a low murmur of
voices. A pair of hands began clapping. Other
hands quickly joined in. A burst of applause
broke over her head and the noise was swelled by
a wave of loud, excited voices. Jenny was jolted
out of her private reverie. She looked up to a sea
of admiring faces and she shrivelled with
embarrassment. Her gaze darted to Tony in
urgent appeal.

'More!' Someone cried, and the cry was taken
up by others, a loud chorus of eager prompting.

'Tony! Stop it!' she begged frantically.

'You were great!' he declared with fervour.

'Please! Do something!'

He sighed and climbed to his feet, shielding
her from view. He held up his hands for quiet,
and expecting their request to be granted, the
crowd hushed.

'Sorry, folks. That was a one only. Be good
people and back off now. You're distressing the
lady and she's given you a great memory.'

There was some protest but most people

accepted his word good-naturedly. Jenny felt hopelessly self-conscious.

Tony turned back to her with a smile. 'That was out of this world, Jenny-wren.'

'All I want is to be out of this crowd,' she muttered.

She glanced nervously over his shoulder and saw Robert heading straight for her, hard purpose on his face. A man grasped his arm, halting him for a moment. She cringed at the thought of discussing her song with Robert. In desperate haste she thrust the guitar at Tony, ordered him to take it back, then turned and fled. People hindered her progress, catching at her and mouthing words which were full of superlatives. Her need to be alone and out of the public eye prompted her to dart up the spiral staircase.

She was already past the gallery of paintings and heading down a passageway when Robert's voice made her falter. He had followed her. Jenny did not know what to do. Her emotions were too dangerously close to the surface. If she had to face him they might get out of control. She rushed onward in a bid to escape.

A hand closed over her shoulder, pulling her to a halt. 'Jenny . . .' Her name was a taut demand. He turned her around.

She could not bring herself to look at him. Her breath came in harsh gasps. Even his touch frightened her. Weakness was invading her limbs. She felt like jelly and there was no strength she could call on.

'Your song! Why didn't you let me know?'

His breath was coming harshly also. She stared at his chest as it heaved up and down. When she made no reply his fingers dug into the soft flesh of her upper arms and his voice carried a note of desperation.

'Jenny . . .'

'When? When could I let you know?' she spilled out in a frantic rush. Then in a flash of counter-accusation, 'You never gave me any time.'

'Time,' he grated out as if the word angered him. 'I had to let you have time. But your song, Jenny . . .' He drew in a shuddering breath. 'Why did you sing it like that? You looked at me . . .'

'And I made you look at me,' she snapped, almost at the end of her tether. Her eyes lifted to his and showed her pain. 'You didn't even want to know me tonight.'

Pain answered her. 'Not know you,' he hissed. 'God almighty! If you knew . . .' His hand slid from her shoulder to the back of her neck, grasping it possessively.

Jenny opened her mouth to protest. He silenced her with a kiss which demanded her surrender. It was an invasion intent on plundering all that she had to give and Jenny recoiled from it. She could taste the whisky he had consumed and it revolted her. There was no tenderness, no love. She pushed at him with what little strength she had.

His assault on her mouth was withdrawn, but his lips pressed a fiery trail of kisses around her face as words were muttered with rough urgency. 'Don't fight me. Please, Jenny. Please . . . I've got to be right. It was in your song. Don't deny me now. You looked at me.'

His head lifted and his eyes burnt down at her

with a feverish hunger. Her lips parted in a soft
sigh as her own need rushed to meet his. And
they kissed, passion fusing with passion. Her
head whirled with a thousand re-awakened senses
as he turned with her and pressed her hard
against the wall, his body almost crushing hers.
His hands moved slowly, savouring the curves of
thigh, hip and waist, lingering possessively, then
taking as his own the soft roundness of her
breasts. And his mouth never left hers, claiming
all its sweetness with seductive mastery, insisting
that she was his and only his.

With shocking swiftness they were wrenched
apart. Jenny sagged, her legs trembling with an
aching weakness. She pressed back against the
wall for support, gasping for breath. In a daze she
saw Tony throw Robert against the opposite wall
and hold him there by the throat.

'I ought to tear you apart,' he grated out
menacingly.

Violence flared from Robert's eyes. There was
a dangerous moment of incredible tension which
seemed to last forever.

'Don't come the heavy with me, Tony,' Robert
warned with equal menace. 'You might have the
muscle but I have the skills, remember.'

'Skills get blurred with alcohol, big brother,
and your breath reeks of it,' Tony retorted but he
released his grip. 'Groping Jenny like she was one
of your two-bit stars. That was a rotten thing to
do!'

Dark, turbulent eyes swept over Jenny. Her
fear of violence was still stamped on her face.

'Oh Christ!' It was a deep, rasping groan and
he covered his face with his hand. The fingers

slowly dragged down his cheeks and he fixed his
gaze on Tony. 'Put it down to the drink. It makes
fools of all of us.' His mouth twisted with sour
mockery. 'After all, you know virgins aren't my
style. An aberration of the moment, Tony.'

He patted his brother's shoulder and walked
away from them, swaying a little as if not quite in
control of himself. Tony expelled a long breath
and gathered Jenny in with gentle hands, tucking
her against him for support. She was still shaking
and Robert's last statement had curdled the
passion he had so deliberately stirred.

'Come and I'll sit you down somewhere while I
get the car-keys from Rob. We're going home.
He is over the brink, Jenny. That's not normal
behaviour from him, not in a public place. I'd
better warn Miranda to pour him into a taxi
before she leaves. She can get any number of men
to bring her home.'

Jenny made no protest to any of Tony's plans.
She was only too grateful to fall in with them.

CHAPTER NINE

TEARS oozed silently from beneath her thick eyelashes and Jenny made no attempt to stop them or wipe them away. Her control had been shattered and she had lost the grit to paste it back together. Tony drove more sedately than usual, his silence and carefulness telling her more strongly than words that he was well aware of her distress. When he finally garaged his father's car he turned to her with a heavy sigh.

'Some bloody night you've had! First me and then Rob getting at you. I'm sorry, Jenny. Sorry I went for Rob like that too. You must have felt dreadful, me tearing him off you and leaving you just standing there.' He shook his head regretfully. 'But I had to interfere. You looked so helpless and he . . .'

'Don't say any more, Tony,' she whispered huskily. 'Let's go inside.'

Tony helped her out of the car and escorted her right up to her room. He opened her door, then dropped a light kiss on her forehead. 'We'll be home tomorrow,' he murmured as if it should be some consolation to her. He touched her cheek in a light caress and gave her a smile. 'Just go to sleep and try to forget that tonight ever happened.'

He turned to go and all the painful confusion in Jenny's heart bubbled up her throat and erupted in a hoarse cry. 'Don't leave me!' She desperately needed to hold onto someone because she was falling apart and nothing made any sense any more. Out of the maelstrom of warring emotions had come one thought. She did not want to be a virgin. Somehow it made her less of a woman.

Tony frowned, hesitated, then stepped inside her room and shut the door behind him. He took hold of her upper arms and searched her face intently. 'You really are shaken up, aren't you? Come on. I'll put you to bed and sit with you for a while.'

A wild hysteria burst across her brain and found voice in derisive laughter. She threw off his hold and backed away from him, her hands flying around in uncontrolled gestures as she panted out the necessary words.

'I don't want you to sit with me. Or talk. Or be kind. I want you to make love to me. You said . . . you said I was desirable. Remember? Well, desire me then. I want you to.'

Her fingers found her zipper and pulled it down. She stepped out of her dress. Her eyes demanded that he not turn away from her as she stripped off her underclothes and stood defiantly naked before him.

'This is how you like me, isn't it? Completely natural? Nothing but me. You want me like this, don't you? Don't you?' she cried pleadingly as he made no move towards her. Tears swam into her eyes again and her proud stance crumpled. 'Please, Tony,' she sobbed and bent her head in abject submission. 'I need you . . . I need you . . .'

Warm arms enfolded her and her face was pressed against a wildly thumping heart. One hand roughly stroked her hair while the other arm tightened the embrace, straining her closer. The hard tension of his body left her in no doubt of his arousal. Then a long sigh wavered through her hair as he laid his cheek on the top of her head.

'Jenny love, it would be so easy to take you. Believe me. You are very, very desirable. And maybe I'm crazy for even hesitating, but right now, I don't think you know what you're doing.'

'I do. I do,' she sobbed, winding her arms around his waist and clinging tightly to him. 'I don't want to be a virgin any more,' she babbled into his chest. 'I want you to show me. Teach me how to please a man, Tony. I want you to.'

A shudder ran through him as her body pressed more urgently to his. Then he was forcibly thrusting her away, holding her at arm's length, his face twisted in torment. 'God damn you, Jenny! It's Rob you want, isn't it? Isn't it?' He shook her angrily. 'And you'd use me like that! Just want am I supposed to be? A male whore? A piece of flesh that can give you experience? Is that all I am to you?'

Confusion whirled in painful circles around her head and she saw him through a veil of bitter tears. 'I didn't think you'd mind. You've had so many girls. Why not me? What's wrong with me?' she cried despairingly.

'Because . . . because . . .' He made a strangled sound and flung her away from him.

She hit one of the bed-posts and crumped onto the floor. Unbearably wounded by yet another rejection, Jenny hugged her knees against her chest and rocked herself in wild, unreasoning

grief, lost and floundering hopelessly in an inner
world of pain. A hand touched her shoulder and
she jerked violently from the contact.

'Go away! You don't want me. No one does,'
she sobbed, wallowing in self-pity and hating the
whole world.

A sharp slap on her face brought her back to
quivering sanity. She stared at Tony's grim face
in horror. With a muttered expletive he scooped
her up in in his arms and cradled her roughly
against his chest. He strode purposefully to the
bed and flung back the top covers. She was
unceremoniously dumped onto the cool sheet.
Tony began unbuttoning his shirt. Suddenly
frightened of what she had so hysterically set into
motion, Jenny turned her head into the pillow.

'Look at me!' Tony ordered in a tight voice
which whipped across her fears, sharpening them
into pain.

She looked. Her gaze skipped up from the
hands at his belt buckle, above the bare expanse
of muscular chest to the hard resolve on his face.
The blue eyes held her relentlessly.

'I won't let you hide your face, Jenny, nor close
your eyes. The light will remain on. You won't
be able to pretend it's Rob or anyone else but me.
And don't think tonight will see it finished. We
live together, remember. Once I share your bed I
won't be content to go back to a platonic
relationship, you to your bed, I to mine, because
I won't be able to forget, and neither will you.'

He unzipped his trousers and stepped out of
them. Jenny grew cold and rigid as his words
chilled her, each one stabbing an icy spray of
sanity into her mind.

'I'll teach you what you want to know, but don't think I'll then stand back and watch you go to someone else. You're not an easy-come easy-go proposition, Jenny. If you give yourself to me, I'll keep you.' He drew in a sharp breath and his eyes glittered with some indefinable emotion. 'I've told you what you're doing. Now, tell me you still want me to make love to you.'

'No.' The word wavered out, a whisper between stiff lips.

Jenny swallowed convulsively. It was necessary to get a grip on herself. Tony stepped closer and she flinched as one hand seemingly reached for her. It slid under the pillow and pulled out her nightie.

'Put it on,' he said flatly and turned away.

A flush of shame brought tingling life to her veins. She hurriedly donned the flimsy garment and pulled the bedclothes up around her neck. She darted an embarrassed glance at Tony. He had his trousers on again. His shirt was flung carelessly over one shoulder.

'I'm . . . I'm sorry, Tony,' she stammered. 'I guess . . . I guess I went a bit crazy.'

'Yeah.' He sighed heavily and gave her a derisive look. 'Guess I went a bit crazy too. Fact is, Jenny-wren, it's been that kind of night, right from the time you appeared like something out of the Arabian Nights. It was all for Rob's benefit, wasn't it? The dressing up . . . and the song.'

She nodded and look down at her blunt, practical fingernails. 'You were right though. It was stupid of me to even try to compete.'

'Not as stupid as me. Maybe I didn't want to see what was there to see. You weren't exactly fending Rob off when he was groping you at the party.' He rubbed a weary hand across his face. 'Of all men to fall in love with, you had to go and pick my brother.' He began walking towards the door, shaking his head as he went. 'And he's no good for you, Jenny. No good at all.'

'Why?' It was a cry of protest, wrenched from her aching heart.

Tony leaned his head against the door for a moment, then flicked off the light. She thought he was leaving but he walked back to her bed, a looming figure in the darkness, a mocking voice which carried a tinge of sadness.

'You know why, Jenny. Think how he's twisted you around already, making you try to be something you're not. You're a very special person in your own right. If he doesn't love you as you are, what kind of happiness can you find with him?' He sighed and continued heavily. 'You know why he doesn't want a virgin? He's used to sex without responsibility and he couldn't take you and shrug you off like all the rest. Only a fool could. And Rob's not a fool. He's attracted to you. I wasn't so blind that I couldn't see that. But he's grown too cynical to commit himself to one woman. Your love for him is a lost cause, Jenny.'

Tears were slowly rolling out of the corners of her eyes. Tony brushed her cheek with his fingertips and felt their wetness.

'Oh hell! Move over,' he muttered and climbed into bed with her, hugging her tightly against his chest and stroking her back in soothing comfort.

His body seemed to envelop her with warmth and Jenny slowly relaxed in his embrace, accepting his compassionate impulse for what it was, one person responding to another's distress. They lay in silence for a long while. Only the slight whisper of Tony's rhythmic caress on her long hair made any sound.

'I'm glad we're going home tomorrow,' she murmured wearily.

His hand stopped moving and she felt his chest expand as he drew in a deep breath. He exhaled slowly.

'No. We won't be going home. Not tomorrow. Nor the day after. We have to stay now,' he said in a tightly determined voice.

'But why?' she asked in bewilderment.

He did not answer.

Jenny pushed herself up enough to look into his face. It was a dark silhouette, telling her nothing. 'You said you wanted to go, Tony,' she reminded him.

'That was before . . . not now.' He stroked her cheek and his eyes seemed to glitter in the darkness. 'I thought . . . I thought so many things.'

The lonely desolation in his voice stabbed through Jenny's own fog of misery. 'Tell me,' she invited softly wanting to soothe his pain as he was soothing hers.

He stirred restlessly, moving away from her and putting his hands behind his head. 'I thought you needed a change, Jenny. You were only existing, not really aware of people. Like you were suffering a long hangover from your father's death. I thought coming here to my family might wake you up. I just didn't anticipate that Rob . . . that you'd be attracted to Rob. I wanted to make you happy . . .' He turned towards her. One hand reached out and cupped her face. 'And be damned if I'll take you home and watch you pining for him. It's got to be resolved.'

Jenny lay back down with a deflated little sigh. 'What's to be resolved? You heard him. He doesn't want me.'

'But you still want him.'

'I can't help that.'

There was a short silence. Then Tony rolled towards her, lifting his head to look down at her face. One hand gently pushed the hair away from her temples. 'Maybe I could help if you let me, Jenny,' he said softly, and there was love and need in his voice.

'What . . . what do you mean?' she whispered, her throat suddenly dry. She was awake now, wide awake, her mind reeling with the fact that Tony wanted her, had wanted her all along, only she had been too blind and too self-absorbed to see it.

The overhead light snapped on. Startled by the harsh brightness, both she and Tony looked towards the switch. Robert stood in the doorway, his face stiffly set into a hard, white mask. Only the eyes were alive, two burning coals which seared the couple on the bed and then retreated. The light flicked off. The door closed. A dreadful darkness enveloped them. She and Tony were alone again, yet not alone. Robert's presence sliced between them, a forceful wedge which drove them apart.

'I'll kill him!' Tony muttered, flinging off the bedclothes and erupting out of the bed.

'No!'

Jenny grabbed for him in vain. Tony was across the room in a couple of bounds, wrenching the door open, calling after Robert.

'Just what the hell do you think you were doing?'

Jenny held her breath. There was no answer. Then Tony was gone. A loud thump was followed by a scrabbling sound and hoarse breathing. With her heart in her mouth, Jenny scrambled off the bed and rushed to the door.

'Not twice in one night, Tony!'

The low, threatening words came out jerkily. Robert was hunched over as if fighting for breath. Tony was sprawled on the carpet at the far end of the corridor.

'You keep away from Jenny, do you hear?' Tony growled as he staggered to his feet.

Robert moved forward, his body tensed, menace in every step. 'You hypocrite! You bloody hypocrite! I could kill you as soon as look at you. No games, you said. She's not for playing with, you said. Well, what goddamned tune have you been playing, Tony?'

'And what did you have in mind when you opened the door?' Tony retorted savagely as he dropped into a defensive crouch.

'Stop it!' Jenny cried, desperate to prevent the imminent violence.

She might not have spoken. Both men ignored her.

'I was looking for you, little brother.'

'Like hell you were looking for me!'

Tony hurled himself forward. Robert seemed to ride with the attack, leaning backwards and twisting aside. It was Tony who finished up on the floor.

'You took advantage of her, didn't you, you bastard?' Robert spat at him.

'So what if I did!' Tony snarled back. 'You were the one who screwed her around so much she didn't want to be a virgin any more.'

'Tony!' Jenny cried in anguished protest.

But he was not listening. His arm snaked out and jerked Robert's feet from under him. The two men were wrestling with vicious intent when Edward Knight's voice rang down the corridor, whip-like in its sharpness.

'Enough! Robert! Tony! Get away from each other this minute. I will not have physical violence in this house.'

Jenny shrank back against the wall as he marched past her, a fearsome figure of authority. His two sons dragged themselves apart and staggered to their feet, still glowering hatred at each other. Edward Knight subjected each to a contemptuous stare, then made a sharp gesture of disgust.

'Go to your rooms. And stay there for the rest of the night. I'll speak to you both in the morning. And mark me well. I expect sanity to prevail or you'll both be out on your ears.'

Neither Robert nor Tony moved.

Edward Knight stepped first to one bedroom door and then the other, flinging them open. 'I'm warning you. If I'm not obeyed immediately you'll answer to your mother.'

Tony surrendered first. He swung on his heel and strode into his room, slamming the door after him.

Edward Knight turned to his eldest son. 'You surprise me, Robert,' he bit out angrily.

'Perhaps I surprise myself,' came the muttered retort. Then he turned, too, disappearing into his room and closing the door in a hardly more restrained manner than his younger brother.

Edward Knight's shoulders slumped as he expelled a deep sigh. Jenny wanted to slink into her room and escape his censure, but there was no ultimate escape. She was a guest under his roof and he would think even more poorly of her if she scuttled away like a coward. He turned and his step seemed to drag as he walked towards her. She forced herself to meet his gaze. His expression was grim.

'I'm sorry, Mr Knight,' she whispered.

His eyes swept over her in silent condemnation. 'I'm sorry too, Jenny. I had you figured differently and I'm extremely disappointed to find my judgment astray. Goodnight. And may I suggest that you'd do well to remain in your room also,' he added cuttingly.

Tears blurred her eyes but Edward Knight did not see them. He had already dismissed her. She watched in silent misery as he plodded down the corridor to his own bedroom. He did not look back. The firm shutting of his door echoed like a death-knell to Jenny's hopes of ever belonging to this family. Edward Knight would not forgive her for causing a rift between his sons. And yet she had not meant to do so. In a few violent moments everything had changed.

Feeling totally wretched in body and spirit Jenny trudged back to bed. She lay in the darkness, facing up to the truth that nothing could be the same again. Her relationship with Tony had been irrevocably altered. Living in the same house would be impossible now that she knew how he felt. There would be too many tensions. And she herself had changed. She was no longer the innocent, inexperienced girl who had arrived at this house.

Now that she looked back, she recognised the many signals which should have revealed Tony's feelings; the insistent invitation to meet his family, his possessive manner which had triggered everyone's assumption that she was his girl, the kiss on her first night here, a host of things in his words and manner to her. How carelessly she had overlooked those signals! Her mind had been preoccupied with Robert, always Robert, from the moment they had met.

Her memory fastened on the scene by the pool on Boxing Day. Tony had been warning his brother off, not protecting her as she had thought. And Robert had backed off, very abruptly. She wondered now if Tony had said more to his brother in private. Not that it mattered. Robert could not have felt as strongly as she or he would not have conceded so readily to Tony's claim on her.

Tonight . . . tonight had been disastrous in so many ways. Jenny's mind shied away from examining it closely. The memories weighed too heavily on her heart. There were several stark truths which she could not ignore or gloss over. She could not give Tony what he wanted and Robert was not prepared to give her what she wanted. To stay on here would only cause more dissension and unhappiness. Jenny was too fond of the Knight family to risk straining the bonds of affection which held them together. Whatever damage she had unwittingly caused tonight would soon be healed if she removed herself. She had to go.

CHAPTER TEN

JENNY stood at her bedroom window and watched Edward Knight. He pottered around the garden beyond the swimming-pool, stooping occasionally to pull out a weed or pausing to examine a plant. He seemed at peace with himself, but Jenny could not quite believe his thoughts were peaceful. What lay behind the calm facade disturbed her so much that she was still postponing the inevitable meeting with him.

It was eleven o'clock. The house was quiet. Jenny wondered what the rest of the family was doing, if Tony and Robert were still in their rooms. She did not want to see them now that her mind was made up to go. She glanced around her room with dull, listless eyes. Everything had been packed. The bed was neatly made. There was nothing left to do but speak to Edward Knight.

Screwing her courage to the necessary sticking point, Jenny walked out of her room, down the stairs and straight outside. Her footsteps seemed to ring loudly on the paving stones around the pool. It was a beautiful morning; blue, cloudless sky, bright sunlight glittering off the water. It was a morning which should have been greeted with pleasure, but the gloom in Jenny's heart cast too great a shadow.

She had dressed in a neat, tailored trouser suit, ready for travelling. The light apple-green of the linen looked fresh and cool but Jenny did not feel cool. Her skin was clammy with nervous tension, her mind feverish with the futile search for suitable words. She rounded a stand of crêpe myrtles and, too suddenly, came face to face with Edward Knight.

'I . . . I have to speak to you,' she stammered.

He nodded. To her intense relief he showed no sign of the harsh condemnation which had hardened his eyes last night. She spoke in a rush, stumbling over the words.

'I can't . . . there's . . . there's a night train I can catch. You must see that I can't stay any longer . . . that I have to go. I'm sorry . . . deeply sorry about what happened last night. It's just . . . it's best that I go. I'm all packed. I'll call a taxi.' Her voice wobbled as tears welled up in her eyes. She swallowed and blinked rapidly, desperate to keep control long enough to say goodbye. 'Thank you for your kind hospitality. Please say goodbye to everyone for me and tell them I'm sorry . . . very sorry that . . .'

'Jenny, I'm not sure that any good purpose will be served by your running away.'

The heavy sadness in his voice prompted more tears. They trickled through her lashes and she had to bite her lips to keep back the sobs which formed lumps in her throat. Speech was impossible. She shook her head and turned away.

'Don't go, my dear. There's no hurry to catch your train and in any case, I would insist on seeing you on to it personally. Stay and talk with me for a while. I think we have much to talk about.'

She dashed the wetness from her cheeks and gulped in a few deep breaths. Her mind urged her to go but her heart cried out for a stay of judgment.

An arm slid around her heaving shoulders, squeezing them in sympathetic comfort. 'Here!' A clean handkerchief was thrust into her hand. 'You haven't given me time to apologise for leaping to hasty conclusions last night, and I do apologise, Jenny. Come. We'll stroll around the garden and perhaps we can work out what should be done.'

He drew her along with him, setting a slow, leisurely pace. 'I'm very fond of roses. They're at their best at this time of year. Annabel has a liking for these creamy ones with the delicate, pink tips, but I prefer the traditional red rose. See the dark velvet of this one? Beautiful, isn't it?'

Jenny nodded, thankful that he was giving her time to recover her composure. His calm, unhurried manner was soothing to her ragged nerves.

'You know, Jenny, when Tony brought you home to us you reminded me of an unopened rose. You breathed the promise of a very special beauty. All you needed was the warmth of love to coax you into spreading your petals and meeting life to the full. Perhaps I'm getting old and sentimental. When I watched you play the song you'd composed for your father, I thought how much I'd like to welcome you into my family as a daughter.'

They had paused in front of a graceful weeping rose. Edward Knight sighed and Jenny felt forced to make some answer.

'You're very kind and I'm grateful . . .'

'No, not kind,' he interrupted gently. 'Just an

old man's fancy. See this rose, Jenny. It's taken seven years to train it into its symmetrical shape. Sometimes patience is rewarded with the results one wants. Patience and determination. The question is . . . what do you want, Jenny? Do you know?'

She hesitated, tempted to confide in him, yet knowing in her heart that it would not change the situation. 'Mr Knight, I remember my first day here too. Tony and Robert greeted each other with warm affection. I'm a thorn in the midst of this family, not a rose. I want . . . I want it to be like it was between them. If I go now . . .'

He shook his head. 'Last night they were at each other's throats. This morning I tried to speak to each one of them. They are both tight-lipped except on one common point. You are completely innocent of provoking the argument between them. It follows then that your going away will not mend the breach, Jenny. It may very well widen it.'

She looked at him with eyes which reflected all her mental anguish. 'What can I do? It's all so hopelessly mixed up.'

'Is it?' he asked softly. 'Do you love one of my sons?'

It was such a direct question there was no way to evade it. 'Yes,' she breathed despairingly. 'I didn't know it could happen like this. That love could be such an obsession, blotting out everything else. I thought of love as happiness. But it's not. It's not like that at all. It's a terrible . . . terrible emotion, twisting and tearing, hurting . . .'

'Not always, Jenny. It can be the most

wonderful thing of your life. Unfortunately it
sometimes does bring unhappiness and I'm afraid
it's probably inevitable in this case. But there can
be no question of your leaving us. The friction
between my sons will eventually smooth out, and
whatever the future brings, I'll welcome you as a
daughter and I hope you'll consider me a father.'

'Mr Knight, you don't understand,' she forced
out in an agony of embarrassment. 'He doesn't
want to marry me. For him it's only . . . he . . . he
only wants to . . . to . . .' She drew in a
shuddering breath and spoke in a determined
rush. 'It won't solve anything if I stay.'

He took her hands and squeezed them
reassuringly. 'You're mistaken about that, I'm
sure. A man's passions can be difficult to control
when he loves deeply. I've never seen Tony
so . . .'

'No!' It was a cry of torment as she realised he
had fastened on the wrong son. 'Mr Knight, I
know that Tony cares for me. That's what makes
it so hard. I don't love Tony. I never will. Not in
the way he wants. I'm very, very fond of him
but . . .'

'It's Robert,' he sighed, and it was a heartfelt
sigh of relief. 'Well, thank God for that. And
light has finally dawned.' He suddenly smiled at
her, and the smile grew into pure, undiluted
pleasure. 'My dear Jenny, you've just taken a
hundred years off my already advanced age. I had
grave doubts that a marriage between you and
Tony would prove successful, but Robert is an
entirely different proposition.' He drew her arm
through his and began walking again with more
of a spring in his step.

Jenny was completely bewildered by his manner. He was acting as if everything was going to be all right and that simply was not the case.

'Ah yes!' he exclaimed with satisfaction. 'That certainly changes the complexion of things. What we now need is a masterly campaign. I think you can safely leave that in my hands. Do you play chess, my dear?'

'Yes, but . . .'

'Then I think we shall spend the afternoon playing chess. Give my sons time to cool down. With you removed from the combat zone and under my protection, they shall have to stop and think, won't they? They might even re-open lines of communication. One can always hope.'

The relish in his voice plunged Jenny into further confusion. 'Mr Knight, I shall be happy to play chess with you but I don't think . . .'

'Trust me.' He patted her hand in a fatherly manner. 'It will be all right. I know my sons.' He stopped walking and took a deep breath as if the air had suddenly turned sweeter. Then his expression of well-being was abruptly dimmed by a frown. He darted an anxious look at her. 'There is the matter of last night. I know these things happen. Perfectly understandable. But if Tony was persuasive . . .'

A hot tide of shame scorched across her cheeks.

Edward Knight squeezed her hand. 'Now, now, it doesn't change a thing, just creates a slight difficulty . . . which shall be overcome. Robert is no romantic fool. Above all he is a realist. Not to worry . . .'

'Please stop,' Jenny begged. Her eyes pleaded for understanding because honesty demanded that he be told everything. 'I think you should know what's been happening. You might change your mind and not want me to stay.'

His keen gaze probed her torment. 'I won't change my mind, Jenny, but perhaps you need to tell me for your own sake. We'll sit down. There's a garden bench just over here.'

The sympathetic caring on his face encouraged her to begin and with only an occasional hesitation, she spilled out the whole truth, what she had thought, her feelings, her misconceptions. When it was all told she raised troubled eyes to her silent confidante. 'So you see, Mr Knight, Tony and Robert lied to you. I'm not innocent. If I hadn't . . .'

'No. They didn't lie,' he interrupted with calm certainty. 'Human relationships hang on such twisted threads. So many things get in the way, distorting what should be direct lines of communication. I'm sorry that you've been hurt badly, Jenny, and you're not to reproach yourself for anything that's happened.' He sighed and gave her a wry little smile. 'Much as I deplore violence, perhaps it has forced my sons to face up to some truths within themselves. We shall tread softly, my dear, and await developments. Abide by me.'

'Dad?' It was Miranda's voice.

'Over here,' he called.

'Lunch is ready. Is Jenny with you?'

'Yes. We're coming now.' His eyes twinkled mischievously at Jenny as they stood up. 'I think I shall pick you a rose. Yes, a full-blooded, red rose. It appeals to me. And it will be a subtle reprimand to my sons who have thought mainly of themselves and given far too little consideration to you.'

'I'll feel silly holding a rose,' she demurred, feeling shy from having revealed so much.

'Nonsense!' he grinned. 'You can fiddle with it, smell it, examine it. A rose is a splendid aid at the table when you find the company a strain.'

He picked a perfect specimen and handed it to her. She smiled her appreciation of the gesture.

'You see? It's made you feel better already.'

He tucked her arm into his and escorted her to the dining-room with all the aplomb of a man in total control of the situation. The rest of the family was already seated. Tony jumped up to hold out her chair and Jenny slid into place with a murmured 'thank you'. Mrs Cherry bustled in and placed a carving dish of roast meat in front of Edward Knight.

'Ah! Perfect timing, Mrs Cherry,' he said with a mischievous roll of the tongue.

'If you say so, Mr Knight. Roast pork can always stand a bit of extra cooking. Mind the crackling though. It's very crisp.'

'Mmm ... smells marvellous!' He glanced brightly around the table. 'I hope everyone has a good appetite. It's a glorious day outside, Annabel. I've been showing Jenny the garden.'

'You must have said all the right things, Jenny,' Miranda remarked teasingly. 'Dad's a miser with his roses.'

'It's lovely, isn't it?' Jenny murmured, twirling it slowly around to view it from all angles. Edward Knight had been right about its usefulness. She could not bring herself to look at Robert or Tony.

'Did you enjoy the party, Miranda?' her father asked interestedly.

'Mmm ... had a fantastic night! Though I must say, for two people who were going to melt into the crowd, Jenny and Tony sure did their things! Now don't blush, Jenny. Your song was great. Everyone said so. The trouble was, they all wanted to know who you were and where you came from. I must have answered a thousand questions once I let on I knew you.'

'I'm sorry,' Jenny muttered self-consciously. 'I didn't mean ...'

'Don't apologise. I basked in the limelight. Your song was a real show-stopper. I've just been telling Mum all about it.'

'And it was the "Wishing" song!' Annabel Knight exclaimed with warm pleasure. 'Congratulations, Jenny. I wish I'd been there to hear it. What did you think of it, Robert?'

Jenny lifted the rose, ostensibly to smell its perfume but hoping it would hide the rush of colour to her cheeks.

'To use your own word, Mother, it was haunting. Unforgettable.' The words were quietly spoken in a toneless voice.

'Well, I say it's the best song I've ever heard,' Tony declared aggressively, as if daring anyone to deny it.

Jenny blessed Mrs Cherry's timely reappearance. Dishes of hot vegetables were passed around the table. The meat was served on warm dinner-plates and there was a lull in conversation as everyone attended to the meal.

'What I want to know is what you said to Cassandra Flemming, Tony,' Miranda opened up again, blithely unaware of any tension.

'Cassandra!' Tony muttered derisively. 'Medusa suits her better.'

'Tony, you didn't!' his mother chided.

'Well, I ask you! What can a woman like that expect? Hair stuck out everywhere like she'd had an electric shock. And the make-up! Talk about a creature from outer space, as Pete would say.'

'Don't drag me into it,' Peter was quick to protest. 'Pass over the extra crackling please, Rob.'

'Making a pig of yourself as usual,' Tony sliced back at him.

'Tony!' It was a sharp reprimand from his mother.

'What's the matter with you?' Miranda said impatiently. 'You're like a bear with a sore head. Had too much to drink, I suppose. It's just as well Cassandra didn't take offence. She is the studio boss's daughter, you know.'

'So?'

It was frustration that was shortening Tony's temper. Jenny could feel him seething with it. She darted a wary look at Robert. He was concentrating on his meal, ignoring everyone. She glanced at Edward Knight. His lips twitched in a slight smile.

'I seem to recall that Cassandra Flemming is an artist,' he said archly.

'She's made a name for herself,' his wife commented. 'I wouldn't call her a serious artist, Edward, but she's clever.'

'Clever!' Tony scoffed and proceeded to spout forth a scathing indictment of her work.

His mother frowned but it was his father who came up with a pointed remark.

'Sounds as if Miss Flemming got under your skin, Tony.'

'Well, he certainly got under hers,' Miranda said slyly. 'She wanted to know all about him.'

'God! I hate women like that,' Tony declared contemptuously.

'Why?' Jenny asked, curiosity prompting her to speak. 'I admired her. She was so self-assured.'

It had been a mistake to draw attention to herself. Both Robert and Tony looked at her. There was pain in Robert's eyes, a gentle compassion in Tony's. Both expressions cut her to the quick. She immediately dropped her gaze to her plate and neatly arranged her knife and fork side by side.

'You're worth ten of her, Jenny,' Tony insisted softly. 'It was you that everyone applauded last night, not that witch of a woman.'

'All the same, I know what Jenny means,' Miranda put in thoughtfully. 'I bet Cassandra Flemming always gets her way through sheer strength of will.'

'A very interesting lady,' Edward Knight said slowly.

'Lady? Huh!' Tony muttered.

'Oh well! It doesn't look like she'll get her way with you since you're leaving this afternoon,' Miranda commented dryly.

'Leaving?' Annabel Knight frowned.

'I'm not leaving,' Tony assured her. 'We've decided to stay on for a while.'

'And I suppose you've decided that on the spur of the moment too,' Miranda said in exasperation.

'Honestly, Tony! You could have given Jenny some notice. She's got all her bags packed.'

'What! Jenny . . .' He turned to her anxiously.

Jenny tensed. Edward Knight came smoothly to the rescue.

'I've taken the liberty of persuading Jenny to stay on for a while, regardless of your capricious decisions, Tony. In fact, she had kindly agreed to play chess with me this afternoon.'

'Chess!' Tony snarled. 'But I wanted . . .'

The doorbell rang. Mrs Cherry was collecting plates from the table. She looked up and sighed her inability to do two things at once.

'I'll get it, Mrs Cherry,' Robert said quickly.

There seemed to be a hint of relief in his voice. It would have been nice to believe he was relieved that she was staying but Jenny decided it was far more likely that he was glad to have an excuse to leave the table.

'Is anyone expecting a visitor?' Annabel Knight asked expectantly.

No one answered in the affirmative. Peter mischievously suggested that it was probably one of Miranda's tribe of dotty admirers, and Tony backed him up with a few mocking remarks.

'Probably someone collecting for charity,' Edward Knight cut in decisively.

They all looked up in surprise when Robert led in a visitor.

'I don't think you've met my mother and father . . . or my youngest brother, Peter,' Robert said with smooth politeness. 'Mother, Dad, this is Cassandra Flemming.'

CHAPTER ELEVEN

THE brilliant smile held all the confidence in the world. 'How do you do? I do apologise for interrupting your meal. Please don't get up, Mr Knight. It didn't occur to me that I might be calling at an inconvenient time. After the party last night, no one's eating at our household so I'm afraid . . .'

'It's no inconvenience, my dear. Please join us,' Edward Knight welcomed her warmly. 'Robert, another chair. Miranda, move down a little. Come, Miss Flemming. Sit here on my right. I am delighted to make your acquaintance.'

'Thank you. I am equally delighted to make yours.'

Jenny could not help staring. The almost arrogant self-assurance was the same but Cassandra Flemming's appearance was in startling contrast to last night's flamboyance. The shock of red-gold hair had been subdued into a prim French-roll. No cosmetics had been applied to the pale, gleaming face. Her white dress was almost nun-like in its modesty.

As Robert saw to the seating of their visitor Jenny glanced at Tony for his reaction. He was leaning back in his chair, a sardonic little smile twisting his lips.

'Well, well, well,' he intoned mockingly. 'Is this the Miss Flemming who accosted me last night?'

'The one and only,' she replied lightly, her eyes challenging him with mischievous intent. 'I was severely frustrated this morning, Anthony Frederick. I had quite decided to paint my face puce, but despite my vast range of cosmetics, that particular shade eluded me. Rather than compromise—I do hate compromises, don't you?—there was simply no other choice but to do the Vestal Virgin bit and come unadorned.'

'Why come at all?' he drawled.

'Tony!' his mother breathed angrily, then smiled at her new guest. 'Please ignore my son's rudeness. I assure you that . . .'

'It's kind of you to be concerned, Mrs Knight,' Cassandra Flemming interrupted sweetly, 'but your large-footed son is only attempting to be provocative.'

Peter sniggered, Miranda grinned, and Jenny could not help a little smile.

Cassandra continued, unabashed. 'He opened his mouth to such a wide extent last night and poured so much scorn on my artistic efforts, that curiosity drove me to this visit. I simply had to find out if his work was worthy of his words.'

'Too bad!' Tony said with exaggerated regret. 'I'm only home on a visit. I don't happen to have my work with me.'

'There's the landscape you gave us for Christmas,' his father said helpfully. 'It's still in your studio, isn't it, Annabel?'

'Yes. Tony can take you to see it after we've finished lunch,' she replied in the tone of an order more than a suggestion.

'Marvellous!' The word was given a wealth of expression; satisfaction, triumph, and a liberal dash of provocation. 'I shall be extremely interested in it.'

'Well, you won't need sunglasses for viewing,' Tony remarked with an edge of sarcasm.

'Not even green-tinted ones, Anthony Frederick?' came the silky retort.

'The name is Tony.'

'How nice! Mine's Cassandra.'

Tony sucked in a sharp breath and let it out with feeling. Fortunately Mrs Cherry came in with the coffee. Annabel Knight directed its serving, forcing a truce in the battle of words. Edward Knight then proceeded to draw Cassandra out about her own work.

Robert was the first to move. He stood up and politely excused himself from the company. Jenny's hand automatically took up the rose again as he stepped behind his sister and Cassandra Flemming. He paused near his father's elbow. Despite her fixed gaze on the rose Jenny knew he was looking at her. Her skin prickled with awareness.

'Jenny . . .'

She raised guarded eyes, unsure what to expect from him. His expression seemed to project concern and a sense of urgency.

'Will you be spending the whole afternoon with Dad?'

Tony stiffened beside her.

'Yes,' she said hastily, intent on avoiding trouble.

'Was there something in particular you had in mind, Robert?' his father asked casually.

'Not right now. Perhaps later.'

'We'll be in my study,' his father nodded and

switched his gaze to Tony. 'Well, my boy, it would seem you chose to challenge a lady of some wit and circumstance. I hope you keep courtesy to the fore, however much your points of view might differ.' He turned to Cassandra. 'Perhaps, my dear, you might like to stay on and join us for dinner, if you do not find my son too offensive.'

Her eyes danced teasingly at Tony. 'Thank you, Mr Knight. I shall only decline if I find that your son's large feet are feet of clay.'

'I can assure you they're not feet of brass,' Tony muttered darkly.

She smiled, 'How fortunate! Quite clearly you dislike the polished article.'

'Miss Flemming . . .'

'Cassandra.'

Tony huffed a sigh of exasperation and pushed himself to his feet. 'What I have to show may not be an artistic *tour de force*, but it is art.' With a pained little smile he added, 'May I have the pleasure of escorting you to my mother's studio?'

Cassandra rose with ladylike grace. Her gaze swept from Annabel to Edward Knight. 'Thank you for receiving me so very civilly. The pleasure of meeting you makes my visit rewarding, even if other pleasures fall short.'

Miranda tittered. As soon as Tony and Cassandra had departed she fell about, howling with glee. 'Feet of clay! Did you see Tony's face? It was classic! Oh boy! That smart tongue of his has met its match, that's for sure!'

Edward Knight looked down the table to his wife and raised a speculative eyebrow.

'Very interesting,' Annabel commented. 'I might just have to drop into the studio myself.'

'Well, if you ask me, it's a head-on clash between a grumpy bull-dog and a spitting cat,' Peter said with all the disdain of youth. 'Give me model soldiers any day. I'm off to a well-ordered war.'

'And Jenny and I shall wage a war of a different kind . . . across a chessboard,' Edward Knight declared with a dry touch of amusement. He gave Jenny an encouraging nod as he rose to his feet.

The study was quiet and comfortable. It seemed to hold an atmosphere of calm reflection. Unfortunately Jenny found it difficult to concentrate on chess. She was tired from too little sleep and too much nervous wear and tear. Her mind could not plot the necessary moves ahead. After her third successive defeat Edward Knight tactfully declined starting a fourth game.

'I'm sorry,' she sighed. 'I can play better. It's just . . .'

'Too much on your mind,' he nodded.

'I'm afraid so.'

'Don't worry, my dear. I'm hopeful that our Miss Flemming is a Godsend. She strikes at Tony's presiding passion, his art, and she's not a person to be easily shaken off. As a distraction, she's perfect. And she's a very clever woman. Very clever,' he added appreciatively.

'Yes. I wish I was like her,' Jenny said wistfully.

He gave her a wry little smile. 'Most men would find your personality much more attractive, Jenny. As a whole we prefer to be the hunters.

Tony, however, is not inclined to hunt. He prefers to let things happen rather than make them. Unfortunately, by sharing the same house with him, you were under his eye all the time.'

She frowned over his meaning. 'Do you think it's just familiarity with him?'

Edward Knight shook his head. 'Oh no! You have qualities which appeal to him very much. Otherwise familiarity would have bred indifference.'

'He's been like a brother to me. I wish last night had never happened,' she said disconsolately.

'That's because you've grown to depend on Tony's support. I imagine you needed someone to lean on after your father's death. But you had to wake up to his feelings sooner or later, and true maturity comes with learning how to cope with reality.'

'I guess so,' she sighed. 'The trouble is I like him so much.'

'Like is not love.' He paused, then added questioningly, 'You do realise that Robert is far from indifferent to you?'

Her mouth twisted with irony. 'Well, I know he doesn't love me like a brother.'

There was a polite rap on the door and Robert entered without waiting for a summons. He held the door open and ushered in a man whose bright, eager gaze immediately sought and fixed on Jenny.

'I hope you don't mind our interrupting your game, but Keith was very anxious to meet Jenny,' Robert explained in a matter-of-fact voice. 'Keith Allerton, my father and Jenny Ross.'

Edward Knight stood and moved forward to shake the visitor's hand. Jenny rose stiffly to her feet, bewildered by the introduction and uncomfortable in Robert's presence. The stranger turned quickly from Robert's father and grasped her hand in both of his.

'My dear Miss Ross, you are a very talented lady and it is a great delight to meet you. I hope to make our association a long and rewarding one.'

Jenny forced a smile even while wishing that the man would let go of her hand. He was coming on too strong and she wasn't in a receptive mood, especially since his words were so puzzling.

'Please sit down, Mr Allerton,' Edward Knight invited smoothly, and seeing her need to be enlightened, he added, 'Our visitor is in the music business, Jenny.'

'Keith was at the party last night and heard your song,' Robert explained more fully.

Jenny's eyes flicked an acknowledgment towards Robert but did not meet his gaze. The aftermath of that song was too sharp a memory.

Keith Allerton settled into a chair as if intent on a long stay. He was a short man of thick build and middle age. His thinning hair was amply compensated by a luxurious moustache and beard. The brown eyes glinted satisfaction at Jenny as she sat down facing him.

'I was completely enthralled, Miss Ross. Unfortunately you left the party before I could contact you, and even when I discovered your connection with the Knight family, Robert, here, was not in a co-operative mood. However, to get to the point, a songwriter of your calibre does not come along very often, and I do not intend to let you slip past me.'

'I took the liberty of playing an edited tape of your songs to Keith, Jenny,' Robert put in quietly. 'He's interested in buying all of them.'

'You played . . . I don't understand . . .'

'Perfectly straightforward, Miss Ross,' Keith Allerton jumped in. 'Robert knew I was interested. He contacted me this afternoon and asked if I wanted to hear more of your work. Ridiculous question,' he grinned, unaware of any undercurrents.

'And you played all of them. Without asking me,' Jenny said to Robert, her eyes full of painful questions.

He frowned, hesitated, then replied in a strangely hollow voice. 'Not quite all. I didn't play . . . your father's song.' His eyes seemed to suggest that it carried too many personal overtones, for him as well as for her, that it was too intimate a song for an outsider's ear.

'You kept one back?' Keith Allerton protested.

'It's not for sale,' Jenny declared firmly, tearing her gaze away from Robert. One intimate look did not necessarily mean what she wanted it to mean. Robert had confused her too many times, and she still did not understand why he had set this up.

Keith Allerton gestured reluctant resignation. 'If you change your mind . . .'

'No.' Her voice gave him no leeway for argument.

'Then I'll rest content if we can come to an agreement on the songs I have heard. And part of that agreement, Miss Ross, will entail my getting first option on any songs you want to sell in the future. I'm sure we can do business for our mutual profit.'

Jenny took a deep breath and tried to grasp hold of the situation. 'Mr Allerton, your interest is very flattering, but you have rather sprung this on me . . .'

'And you want time to think about it and perhaps talk it over before committing yourself,' he nodded. 'Of course, Miss Ross. Shall we say eleven o'clock in my office tomorrow? Robert will bring you in,' he added as he saw her uncertainty.

Jenny looked to Edward Knight for advice. She was too unsure of Robert's motives to meekly fall in with the suggestion.

'No harm in going, Jenny. You don't have to commit yourself to anything unless it satisfys what you want,' he said with calm deliberation.

She wanted to be with Robert. She wanted to share his world. What Robert himself wanted was a large question mark, but maybe tomorrow would give her some indication. 'All right, Mr Allerton. Eleven o'clock tomorrow.'

'Splendid!' he smiled and rose briskly to his feet. 'Glad to have met you, Mr Knight,' he nodded and turned to Robert. 'I am indebted to you, but no doubt I can repay the debt whenever you wish to call it in.'

Robert's answering smile held a cynical twist. Jenny's heart gave a sick lurch. No doubt Robert would extract some return for the favour. That was how the wheel turned, knowing how to use people. And yet, he had seemed concerned about her reaction. She wished she knew his motives for arranging the deal. The door closed behind the two men and she looked her uncertainty at Edward Knight.

'Why don't you ask him?' he said, reading her doubts with pinpoint accuracy.

She shrugged and gave him a wry smile. 'Can I believe his answer?'

'Yes. Robert doesn't lie.'

Jenny brooded over that reply. It was true that Robert had been brutally honest with her on Christmas Day. She was not sure that she wanted that brand of honesty from him again. It hurt too much. She sighed and dragged herself up out of the comfortable, leather armchair.

'Will you excuse me, Mr Knight? I think I'll go to my room. I didn't get much sleep last night.'

'Don't run away, Jenny,' he advised softly. 'Robert will be back in a moment.'

She frowned. 'What makes you think so?'

'When a man goes to the trouble of creating an opening, he used it,' came the dry reply.

No sooner had he spoken than Robert returned, stepping quickly into the room. His eyes darted to Jenny, searching her face intently.

'Allerton gone already?' his father said with an even drier intonation.

'He's a busy man,' Robert retorted. He shot an urgent look at his father. 'Dad, would you mind . . .'

'I'm sure you have much to discuss,' he nodded, and a faint smile curved his lips. 'I think I'll see how Tony's faring with the fiery Miss Flemming.'

He was gone before Jenny could order her thoughts. She stared helplessly at the door. Edward Knight had deliberately abandoned her to Robert's company and she was not prepared for it, not prepared for it at all.

CHAPTER TWELVE

Robert smiled at her. 'You're going to be a very rich woman.'

She stared back at him, her mind registering the smile and the words but unable to fit them into the context of all that had happened between them. Did he think she cared about being rich? Did success make her more attractive, more acceptable to him? What did his smile mean?

He made an expansive gesture. 'The response to your song last night was overwhelming. Allerton, himself, swore he'd never heard anything like it. You can just about name your own price with royalties to follow. When he heard your other songs this afternoon he was jumping out of his skin to meet you and make a deal. He's at the top of his field, Jenny, a man of very wide experience, and he calls you the greatest talent he's come across in his whole career.'

Jenny did not care what Keith Allerton thought.

Her lack of response puzzled Robert. 'Aren't you pleased?'

Pleased. How could she feel pleased when her heart was a pit of despair? Robert had no comprehension of her feelings. With a dispirited sigh Jenny turned away from him and stepped over to the window. Her gaze wandered over Edward Knight's rose-garden. The blooms were at their best at this time of year. Absolute perfection. Beautiful. I'll never be a rose, Jenny thought despairingly. Whatever promise I had is being stifled right now. She could feel the inner petals of her love shrivelling up into a tight ball. There was no sun to coax them open again. Only the tinsel offering of material success. It held no warmth.

A hand touched her waist. She jerked away, startled out of her reverie by the unexpected contact.

'I said ... aren't you pleased?' Robert demanded tightly.

She looked up into a face which was taut with strain. There was no pleasure in his eyes. They were dark with an intense flow of emotion which had nothing to do with pleasure.

'I don't think it matters,' she answered flatly. 'I'll still be the same person. Being rich doesn't matter.'

He frowned with impatience. 'Don't you see this opens doors for you? It will give you the economic freedom to go and do whatever you like. Buy everything you want. Enjoy all the luxuries that . . .'

'Do you have to relate everything to money and success?' she snapped, frustrated and angry at his lack of perception. 'Of course you do,' she added bitterly. 'You told me straight out that if there's an opportunity to take, you take it. So you saw the opportunity to do business with Keith Allerton and you went right ahead. And no doubt you'll profit by it.'

His hands grasped her upper arms in a punishing grip, fingers digging into the soft flesh. 'Don't you realise I did it for you?' he grated out, strong emotion rasping over tight restraint. He sucked in a quick breath and spoke with more control, his eyes demanding that she believe him. 'I did it for you. I don't need more money. I don't need to get one damned thing out of this deal except what's best for you. That's all I wanted . . . what's best for you.'

Her laugh was a whimper of derision. 'And you've given it to me, haven't you, Robert? You've sold my songs.'

'No,' he cut back emphatically. 'All I've done is given you the opportunity to sell your songs if you wish to. And made damned sure that you'll get the best possible deal that could be arranged. You don't have to sign, and it makes no difference to me, personally, if you do or not. Only one thing is important to me and that's you . . . You,' he repeated with vibrant passion in his voice.

She looked at him in bewilderment. His face was grim, the expression in his eyes too enigmatic for her to decipher. 'I don't understand you, Robert. I don't understand you at all,' she said in total confusion.

His face softened as a faint smile curved his lips. 'No. I don't suppose you do,' he murmured with a touch of wry whimsy.

The hands on her arms gentled their hold, then slowly slid around her back and drew her forward. Jenny did not resist. Robert had always been able to exert a magnetism which forced her pliancy, and at this moment she was mesmerised by the play of emotion on his face. His eyes roamed over her features with almost gloating pleasure, and the touch of his hands was the touch of reverence, as if holding something infinitely precious.

'Such a small slip of a girl. Was it only a week ago that Tony brought you home? A week!' He shook his head in disbelief and his eyes glinted with self-mockery. 'How deceived I was at that first meeting! Just a pleasant little thing, a little shy and self-conscious, but rather sweet. I didn't give you a second thought until I came home that night. Then the scales fell from my eyes and I saw a different Jenny Ross.

'You don't even see the magic you weave and yet it's so strong, so very strong. And the spell you cast is inescapable. You're an enchantress with the power to steal a man's soul and make him a stranger to himself. I've done things this week I would never have normally done, acted completely out of character. All these years I've considered my own interests first, everyone else second. What I want, what I need, what's best for me. I had shaped a world where I had everything taped down to the last millimetre. Then you came along and waved your magic wand and everything changed.'

One hand reached up and gently cupped her cheek. 'This sweet face shone with a glow I'd never seen before. I wanted to take it, own it, experience all its warmth. Only your innocence stopped me, and my whole way of life was condemned by that innocence. It forced me to re-think. It forced me to consider your needs, what was best for you. Suddenly I didn't want to take, but to give. I wanted to give you everything you lacked. And the obvious channel was through your music. The talent was there.

I knew how to tap it, knew what encouragement you needed.'

He sighed and his mouth twisted with irony. 'And I hoped you would look kindly on me again. I wanted to bask in the warmth of your pleasure.'

Pain flickered across his expression and his gaze followed his hand as it moved from her cheek and stroked her hair, tucking it lightly behind her ear and smoothing it back. 'Then Tony revealed that he loved you . . .' There was pain in his voice, too, and when he dragged his gaze back to meet hers, the conflict of warring desires was plain to see.' And you responded to him, Jenny. Not in the way he was patiently waiting for, but with obvious warmth and affection. You had a close understanding. I suddenly realised I'd been interfering with something . . . something which could turn out far better for you than anything I could offer.

'There's a simple goodness in Tony which I don't have. I'd already hurt you. Even tainted your innocence with my greed. Tony had unselfishly given you everything you'd needed from him. And he had found you, Jenny. He'd brought you home to meet his family, and I . . . He's my brother and he loved you. There seemed only one honourable course to take . . . to keep out of the way and give you both the chance to reach a more intimate understanding.'

The hand on the pit of her back pressed her closer. 'But honour was a bitter taste to swallow when I hungered for your sweetness, Jenny. Each night I'd stare at your portrait, torturing myself with what I was missing, and each day it was that little bit harder to stay away from you. And last night . . .'

He hesitated, then plunged on with a hint of desperation. 'Last night you looked at me when you sang and it seemed . . . I felt . . . I felt it was for me. And I had to find out. I had to know.' He slid his hand under her hair to the back of her neck. 'And you responded to me. No matter what happened afterwards. When I kissed you, you responded to me in a way . . . I wasn't mistaken, Jenny, was I?'

The burning desire in his eyes certainly could not be mistaken for anything else. Jenny quivered, knowing that he was going to kiss her and knowing he would seduce the same response from her. She was frightened where that would lead her because Robert was making no promises. He had plucked at her heart-strings like a master musician with his long speech, but he was only calling the tune, not completing it.

'Please . . .' she forced out, frantic to stop his assault on her emotions. 'It's not fair, Robert. You're . . . you're like a hawk . . . you pounce and take what you want . . . and then . . . then you fly away and . . .'

'Don't be afraid of me, Jenny,' he interrupted softly, and his mouth was closer to hers.

Like a hypnotised bird she watched his lips move again, helpless to do anything but wait for him to swoop.

'Don't you realise . . . don't you understand what I've been saying? You fill my world. You are my world. Without you . . .'

The study-door crashed open and Tony appeared like an avenging angel, his golden head thrust forward aggressively, blue eyes flashing the fire of challenge. He closed the door and stood against it, drawing himself up to his full height.

'Get your hands off her,' he commanded, each word clipped out with the promise of retribution if he was not obeyed.

Robert's face tightened. He gently withdrew his embrace and swung around to face his brother.

'I warned you, Rob.' Tony took a threatening step forward then gestured his contempt. 'Do you think I don't know how your mind works? Dad told us about the deal you set up with Allerton. It suits your purpose very nicely, doesn't it? Only I'm not going to let you capitalise on it. I'll kill you before I'll see you use Jenny as you've used your other women.'

'Your self-appointed role of protector doesn't hold much force after last night, Tony,' Robert retorted, cold ice to Tony's fire. 'In any case, it's up to Jenny to make her own choices.'

'Choice!' Tony spat out furiously. He shook his fist at his brother. 'She hasn't got a goddamned chance against your bloody conniving. I'm warning you for the last time. Leave her alone!'

Robert glanced back at Jenny, his eyes probing sharply, a painful uncertainty on his face. Then he moved aside, putting distance between her and the violence which threatened.

'I can't leave her alone and I'm not standing off for you or any other man, brother or not,' he announced with hard determination. 'If I have to fight you for her I will, Tony.'

Tony looked murder at him. His hard, athletic

body seemed to bristle with readiness. Jenny was about to cry out a plea when he suddenly checked himself. A painful conflict twisted across his face. His hands unclenched and stretched out in a gesture of conciliation.

'Rob . . . I've loved you as much as any brother could . . . but what you're doing is so wrong . . . despicable . . . can't you see that? Can't you see that she's different?'

'Yes.'

Tony's face contorted with anger. 'Then damn you to hell!' he cursed and moved forward with vicious intent.

'I love her.'

The fierce declaration stopped Tony in his tracks and stole Jenny's breath away.

'I'm going to marry her.'

'You're what?' Tony got out, his voice strangled with shock and disbelief.

'I don't care what happened last night. I love her and if she'll have me, I'm going to marry her, Tony. Nothing means more to me than having Jenny as my wife,' Robert stated with passionate purpose.

Jenny had no time to recover her wits. Tony swung towards her, an agony of uncertainty on his face. Then Robert turned also and there was no more confusion in her heart. Love blazed out of his eyes, love and need, desperately searching for the answer he wanted.

With a lightning burst of clarity Jenny understood all that he had been saying to her, and more. Hadn't Edward Knight told her on that first night that Robert's one emotional mainstay was his family? He had had no other acquaintance

with love, and the ingrained cynicism learnt from
his casual relationships with women in the past
had fed his self-doubts, making him uncertain
that he was capable of answering Jenny's needs.
He had stepped back, not only out of love for his
brother but because he had not believed enough
in his love for her.

But the love had been there, wanting to reach
out to her. The intimacy which had throbbed
between them on Christmas Day had been no
fantasy and the instinctive understanding which
had flowed while they had worked on her songs
had been a natural extension of that intimacy.
Her defensive caution had inadvertantly strength-
ened Robert's doubts and it was not until she had
sung directly to him, revealing all the pain of her
unrequited love, that he had begun to believe he
could be wrong.

'Are you going to marry him?' Tony dragged
out, as if each word hurt him unbearably.

Jenny turned to the man who could only ever
be her dear friend, knowing she must give hurt
but unable to soften the truth. A rush of
compassion for him made her hesitate. Robert
took an urgent step towards her, his body tense,
and in his eyes was the reflection of all the misery
and despair Jenny herself had suffered through
this long week of self-denial. She could not deny
him now. The anxious little voices of fear and
caution were blotted out by the clamour of her
heart. Her answer held all the inevitability of a
predetermined fate.

'Yes. I love him, Tony.'

Before Jenny had time to draw breath again,
she was crushed against Robert's chest, her face

pressed to a hammering heart which beat out its relief to her. His arms were steel bands around her, proclaiming their intention of never letting her go. The warm breath of a shuddering sigh wavered through her hair as his lips brushed across the top of her head, again and again in an ecstasy of ownership.

'Bloody hell!' Tony muttered. 'I should never have brought her home with me.'

The desolation in his voice pierced Jenny's daze of happiness. She sensed his move to leave and guilt prompted her to strain against Robert's possessive embrace.

'Tony!' she called anxiously.

Robert eased his hold and turned with her. Tony was almost at the door. He looked back at her with wry reluctance.

'I'm sorry,' she forced out, knowing the pain of loss too well for her to let him go without a word.

He made a dismissive gesture. 'Not to worry, Jenny-wren. I'm one of the world's great survivors. Can always be trusted to bob up again.' He shot a look at his brother. 'Guess I owe you an apology, Rob.'

'No. I owe you too much, Tony. I can't say I'm sorry that Jenny chose me, but I do feel for you, brother,' he said with gentle sympathy.

'Yeah.' Tony nodded a few times then attempted a smile which didn't quite succeed. 'Anyway, I'm glad I was wrong about you, Rob. Little brothers hate it when big brothers seem to let them down.'

'I understand.'

Tony hesitated, then added. 'About last night. You misread it, Rob. I've got broad shoulders for crying on, you know. Nothing happened. She was crying for you.'

'Thanks, Tony.' It was a sigh of relief and his arm tightened around Jenny's shoulders.

'Peace?'

'Peace,' Robert agreed on a grateful note.

'I expect to be best man,' Tony said with a trace of his old cockiness.

Robert smiled. 'I suspect you are anyway.'

'Not for Jenny, old son. Mind you look after her now. I'll be her brother too, you know.'

'I'll look after her all my life.'

'Good enough. I'll leave you to it.'

Jenny sighed as the door closed behind him. Robert turned her back into a more gentle embrace this time. He tenderly kissed the troubled expression from her eyes.

'I love you, Jenny Ross,' he murmured fervently.

She raised her lashes, wanting to see the glowing confirmation in his eyes. It still seemed incredible that he should love her ... love her enough to want to spend the rest of his life with her.

'Are you sure you want to marry me, Robert?' she asked cautiously.

'Am I sure!' He laughed and swung her around in his arms with a triumphant exuberance which left no doubt in her mind. 'You said yes, and there's no way I'm going to let you change your mind, Jenny Ross, because you're mine.' He put her down and a look of incredulous wonder stole over his face. 'You're really mine,' he whispered huskily.

And if there had still been any uncertainty in

Jenny's mind, it would have been swept away by the kiss which reinforced his claim. It promised her all the answers to all the secret yearnings of her soul. The emptiness was filled with all the sweet joy of love and the rich bond of sharing was founded on the best foundation of all, the sure knowledge of each other's commitment. They formed a whole entity at last, two fitting halves welding together. For a long time they poured out their feelings with all the pleasure that touch could impart. Words came much, much later, when all the accumulated frustration had been conclusively wiped away.

There was one question which niggled at the edge of Jenny's happiness, and within the security of Robert's arms it was possible for her to ask it. 'Why did you walk away from me last night, Robert? You must have known how I felt.'

'No. I didn't know,' he denied gently. 'I'd completely lost control of my own emotions and I couldn't trust my judgment because I wanted so much to believe that you loved me. When Tony forced me away I looked across at you and saw fear, not love. I thought I'd been wrong. That I'd pressed my own feelings on to you and you didn't really want me at all. Your fear curled my stomach into knots. I said what I had to say to fix it with Tony, so he'd overlook my lapse. I'm sorry, darling.'

'I've always hated violence. It terrifies me,' she explained.

His fingertips stroked her cheek with all the tenderness of love. 'No more violence, I promise you. And I'm sorry about that fight with Tony last night. It was senseless. Stupid. I was feeling

pretty shell-shocked from having seen you in bed
with him and I just exploded when he came after
me.'

'Why did you come to my bedroom?' she asked
curiously.

He smiled. The scene no longer held horror for
either of them. 'I kept remembering how you
kissed me back. It was too real to be fantasy on
my part. So I came home meaning to have it out
with Tony, tell him I meant business with you
and may the best man win, etc. etc. Only he
wasn't in his room. I didn't want him to be in
your room, Jenny, but I had to know. That was
one hell of a moment, my love.'

She reached up and kissed away the memory.
'There was only you, Robert. I've never felt this
way about anyone else. You've held my heart in
your hands almost from the first moment we met.
I wanted you to make love to me, you know,' she
added shyly.

He grinned down at her, brimming over with
happiness. 'You don't know how many times I
wished I had, and to hell with what was right or
wrong. But I'll make it up to you, my darling,
with compound interest.'

And he kissed her with hungry passion which
more than asserted his need for her. It eloquently
expressed a passion that only she could satisfy,
and she rejoiced in her ability to give him this,
give him everything he craved.

'I do beg your pardon. I thought this was a
public room!' Sarcasm edged the shock in
Miranda's voice. 'Of course, some people have no
sense of . . . of loyalty,' she continued, her tone
gathering outrage.

Robert checked Jenny's impulse to pull away
from him and turned a bland face to his sister.
'Not that it's any of your business, Miranda, but
Jenny and I are getting married and this room
was private until you burst into it.'

Miranda's mouth gaped open. 'Married! You?'

'As soon as I can lead her to the altar.'

'You? You're getting married!'

Robert sighed. 'As improbable as that obviously
seems to you, I most definitely am, with haste
and no repentance.'

Miranda recovered. 'Well! I must say you've
both been very sly. And just what are you going
to tell Tony?' she demanded officiously.

'He knows,' Robert answered briefly and to the
point.

'Well!' Miranda huffed again, rather at a loss
until she remembered her errand. 'Well anyway,
Dad sent me to tell you that Mrs Cherry's
serving afternoon tea in Mum's sitting-room.' A
look of unholy glee gathered on her face. 'Not
that you want tea. I can see that. You just stay
here and carry on.'

'Hold it!'

Miranda was already closing the door behind
her but she poked her head back around, her eyes
sparkling with anticipation.

'I thought as much,' Robert said knowingly.
'You keep your mouth shut, Miranda, Jenny and
I will be along in a minute and we'll do the
talking.'

She wrinkled her nose at him. 'Spoilsport!
Besides, Jenny's glowing. They'll all know as
soon as you turn up together.'

'Miranda . . .' Robert started threateningly.

'All right. All right. Suit yourself.'

The door closed with a hint of chagrin.

Jenny looked up at Robert questioningly. 'Does it really show?'

He smiled. 'I hope it'll always show. I'll never tire of that look on your face, Jenny. It's so very beautiful.'

'Beautiful?'

He tilted her chin up and his eyes assured her there was no doubt about it. 'Ready to meet your ready-made family?'

'With you,' she nodded.

'Always with me.'

He hugged her against him and they walked out of the study, inseparably linked in each other's hearts and minds. As they entered Annabel's sitting-room everyone looked up. Jenny blushed self-consciously and Robert used the moment without hesitation.

'Mother, Dad, you're about to acquire another daughter. Jenny has just consented to be my wife.'

'Fan-tastic!' Peter shouted gleefully. 'I'll be able to take over your room, Rob. Good on you, Jenny. I thought he'd never get married and move out.'

'Peter!' his mother chided but her smile belied any reproach. 'I'm so glad you're joining the family, Jenny. And I'm very happy for you, Robert. You've chosen a wonderful girl.'

'Thank you, Mrs Knight,' Jenny murmured, gratified by the warmth of her welcome.

'Well, I think they're secretive beasts. I've had no fun out of this at all,' Miranda complained, but there was no acrimony in her words. She grinned at Jenny. 'You'd better make me bridesmaid or there'll be trouble.'

'You needn't think I'll be a rotten page-boy,' Peter growled.

'Who'd have you, you pimply monster?' Miranda retorted. 'I've told you a thousand times not to eat cake.'

Peter poked out his tongue at her before taking a huge bite of strawberry-cream sponge.

'Come sit with me,' Edward Knight invited, his eyes twinkling pleasure at them.

Cassandra Flemming watched them curiously as they settled on the sofa next to Robert's father. Her gaze lingered on Jenny's face then switched to Robert. 'Congratulations,' she said slowly. 'You always did have a good eye.'

'A good ear,' Tony corrected her dryly. He sent the two of them a look of wry resignation then drew in a deep breath and with an air of decision, turned to the woman next to him. 'I've changed my mind, Cassandra—Goddammit, that's an awful name! I'll have to call you Cass— anyhow, on second thoughts, I might just have enough paintings for an exhibition. How about driving to Nangoa with me tomorrow and you can give me your opinion?'

Surprise was quickly followed by her brilliant smile. 'Love to. If they're anywhere near as good as the landscape I've seen, I can promise you it'll be a sell-out success.'

'Yeah. Well, I guess success could be sweet,' he drawled with a touch of irony.

'Leave it to me,' she assured him confidently and bubbled forth a plan of action which drew the others' attention.

Edward Knight took Jenny's hand and squeezed it with fatherly affection. 'Happy now?' he whispered.

'Yes,' she whispered back, her eyes expressing heartfelt gratitude for all his support and kindly advice.

He smiled his satisfaction then gave a slight nod in Tony's direction. 'Would you like to bet me a rose that I'll have three painters in the family before long?'

Jenny looked in surprise at Tony and Cassandra. 'You think so?'

'Cassandra Flemming has a will of iron. She's been battling his offhandedness all afternoon. Now that he's given her an opening, it's odds on that she'll win.'

'You approve?' Jenny asked, not doubting his perception and wanting Tony to be happy.

He gave a soft chuckle. 'My dear, she's precisely what he needs. Didn't I tell you I know my sons?'

Robert leaned forward. 'What are you two talking about?'

'Rose-gardens, my boy,' his father answered swiftly. 'Since you've finally had the good judgment to pick a prize rose, you really should grow a garden of your own.'

Robert grinned at his father then turned to her, his eyes promising her everything she might desire. 'We'll do whatever Jenny wants.'

The Knight family's circle of love closed securely around Jenny. It was a strong circle, strong with the strength of shared years, brick upon brick of understanding and caring, inde-structable. And she knew that the home she and

Robert would build would be of the same mould, because the foundation was here, the design ready-made, and they had the love and the will to carry it through.

Coming Next Month

871 FINDING OUT Lindsay Armstrong
Happiness eludes a woman who was forced to marry an Australian
businessman in restitution for his brother's death. Yet deep down, she's
sure happiness is what her husband wants.

872 ESCAPE ME NEVER Sara Craven
An English ad agency executive dresses down to show she's not a
frustrated widow—ripe for the taking. But her client sees right through
her defenses—and he likes what he sees!

873 SILENT CRESCENDO Catherine George
An English physiotherapist wonders at her sanity when she falls for a
man whose life seems devoted to melodrama. How can she know when
he's being sincere and when he's only pretending?

874 THE BRIDE SAID NO Charlotte Lamb
Prenuptial jitters are the least of her worries. How could her father have
promised his managing director control of the family firm in return for
marrying her? And the wedding is only a day away....

875 ACAPULCO MOONLIGHT Marjorie Lewty
Antagonizing a millionaire at an electronics conference in Acapulco is bad
for business. But his conditions for investing in her company leave her
no choice!

876 TOUCH NOT MY HEART Leigh Michaels
This secretary has sent too many flowers to her boss's ex-mistresses for
her to be taken in. So when he needs a temporary fiancée, she agrees—
never thinking that he could touch her heart.

877 KNIGHT'S POSSESSION Carole Mortimer
Fairy tales, knights in shining armor and happy endings are not in her
vocabulary until her fiancé breaks their engagement and her
stepbrother steps in to save the day—by claiming her for himself!

878 LEGACY Doris Rangel
The initial shock of saving the stranger her late husband willed his half of
their Rocky Mountain retreat to is short-lived. Somehow his being there
seems so right—as if it were meant to be.

No one Can Resist...

HARLEQUIN REGENCY ROMANCES

Regency romances take you back to a time when men fought for their ladies' honor and passions—a time when heroines had to choose between love and duty . . . with love always the winner!

Enjoy these three authentic novels of love and romance set in one of the most colorful periods of England's history.

Lady Alicia's Secret by Rachel Cosgrove Payes

She had to keep her true identity hidden—at least until she was convinced of his love!

Deception So Agreeable by Mary Butler

She reacted with outrage to his false proposal of marriage, then nearly regretted her decision.

The Country Gentleman by Dinah Dean

She refused to believe the rumors about him—certainly until they could be confirmed or denied!

Everyone Loves . . .

HARLEQUIN GOTHIC ROMANCES

A young woman lured to an isolated estate far from help and civilization . . . a man, lonely, tortured by a centuries' old commitment . . . and a sinister force threatening them both and their newfound love . . . Read these three superb novels of romance and suspense . . . as timeless as love and as filled with the unexpected as tomorrow!

Return To Shadow Creek by Helen B. Hicks

She returned to the place of her birth—only to discover a sinister plot lurking in wait for her. . . .

Shadows Over Briarcliff by Marilyn Ross

Her visit vividly brought back the unhappy past—and with it an unknown evil presence. . . .

The Blue House by Dolores Holliday

She had no control over the evil forces that were driving her to the brink of madness. . . .

You're invited to accept 4 books and a surprise gift **Free!**

Acceptance Card

Mail to: Harlequin Reader Service®

In the U.S.	In Canada
901 Fuhrmann Blvd.	P.O. Box 2800, Postal Station A
P.O. Box 1394	5170 Yonge Street
Buffalo, N.Y. 14240-1394	Willowdale, Ontario M2N 6J3

YES! Please send me 4 free Harlequin Presents® novels and my free surprise gift. Then send me 8 brand new novels every month as they come off the presses. Bill me at the low price of $1.75 each ($1.95 in Canada)—an 11% saving off the retail price. There are no shipping, handling or other hidden costs. There is no minimum number of books I must purchase. I can always return a shipment and cancel at any time. Even if I never buy another book from Harlequin, the 4 free novels and the surprise gift are mine to keep forever.

108 BPP-BPGE

_____

Name   (PLEASE PRINT)

_____

Address   Apt. No.

_____

City   State/Prov.   Zip/Postal Code

This offer is limited to one order per household and not valid to present subscribers. Price is subject to change.   ACP-SUB-1R

What the press says about Harlequin romance fiction...

"When it comes to romantic novels...
Harlequin is the indisputable king."
—*New York Times*

"...always with an upbeat, happy ending."
—*San Francisco Chronicle*

"Women have come to trust these
stories about contemporary people,
set in exciting foreign places."
—*Best Sellers,* New York

"The most popular reading matter of
American women today."
—*Detroit News*

"...a work of art."
—*Globe & Mail,* Toronto